camp CONFIDENTIAL

D1489018

TTYL

ISBN 0-439-85243-9

Copyright © 2005 by Grosset & Dunlap. All rights reserved. Published by Scholastic Inc., 557 Broadway, New York, NY 10012, by arrangement with Grosset & Dunlap, an imprint of Penguin Putnam Books for Young Readers, a division of Penguin Group (USA) INC. SCHOLASTIC and associated logos are trademarks and/or registered trademarks of Scholastic Inc.

12 11 10 9 8 7 6 5 4 3 2 1   6 7 8 9 10 11/0

Printed in the U.S.A.   40

First Scholastic printing, April 2006

camp CONFIDENTIAL

TTYL

SCHOLASTIC INC.

New York Toronto London Auckland Sydney
Mexico City New Delhi Hong Kong Buenos Aires

chapter

ONE

natalie > SATURDAY

> **<Aries8>:** Natalie! U there?
>
> **<NatalieNYC>:** jenna!!! omg, what's up? camp only ended sat but i miss u so much already. how's home?
>
> **<Aries8>:** Okay. I'm at my dad's—totally boring. Just surfing the Net with Adam.
>
> **<NatalieNYC>:** hi, adam.
>
> **<Aries8>:** He's getting food right now—I had to IM u and say he got a text msg from Simon last night—just saying hi and whatever and then he was like, "I am totally glad to be home—just miss my friends and obviously Natalie."
>
> **<NatalieNYC>:** aww, that's so sweet!!!
>
> **<Aries8>:** Totally. R u gonna keep seeing him?
>
> **<NatalieNYC>:** ?? don't know. ct isn't that far but . . . there's this guy here i had my eye on last year . . .
>
> **<Aries8>:** Really? What's his name?
>
> **<NatalieNYC>:** kyle.
>
> **<Aries8>:** U mentioned him at camp.
>
> **<NatalieNYC>:** got to go—hannah's here, we're

going back-to-school shopping!!! talk to u on the blog! bye!

<Aries8>: Oh yeah, forgot about Julie's blog. I'd luv to go shopping, if I wasn't stuck at my dad's.

<NatalieNYC>: NATALIENYC is unavailable.

Natalie couldn't believe how excited she was to see Hannah. It had only been a couple of months since Hannah had jetted off to Europe and Natalie had boarded the bus to Camp Lakeview, but it felt like a lifetime—and so much had happened in Nat's life that she knew a huge catching-up session was in order. So the obvious thing to do the second she got home from camp? Call Hannah, and invite her to go shopping the next day! Natalie was beyond thrilled to be back in New York City, where no one considered denim cut-offs and a tank top to be the height of fashion.

She'd brought tons of cute summer outfits to camp, but had never worn any of them, except to the camp-wide social events. And school was going to start on Tuesday—the day after Labor Day, she'd officially be in middle school—so she definitely needed new fall clothes. Plus, Hannah had told her about a school social for all incoming sixth-graders on the first Friday back—just one more reason to get a cute new outfit.

Natalie was talking to Jenna online when she heard the door buzzer ring at the Upper West Side apartment where she lived with her mom. She was practically out of the study before she remembered to say good-bye to Jenna, and then she ran down the hallway to the living room, superexcited to see her best friend.

Hannah, wearing a little purple miniskirt and a black top, was standing in the foyer talking to Natalie's mom, who was still in her pajamas even though it was after noon. For the umpteenth time, Nat was reminded of how great it was to be back—she and her mom had brunched on bagels and veggie cream cheese, watched a couple of cartoons, and just taken it easy for the morning. It had been so long since Natalie had slept past seven that her body automatically woke her up—but she'd ignored the internal alarm, rolled over, and promptly fell back asleep.

"Hannah!" Natalie shrieked.

"Natalie!" Hannah screamed. The two girls leapt at each other, hugging ferociously. "Oh my God, it is so good to see you, Nat!" Hannah said. "I thought this day would never come!"

Natalie laughed. "So melodramatic," she said, teasingly. "Some things never change. I'm thrilled to see you, too! But I gotta tell you, seeing your adorable skirt—I'm pretty anxious to get out and get shopping!"

Natalie's mom laughed. "That's my girl." She crossed the living room and picked up her purse from the red easy chair, which was Natalie's favorite place in the house to curl up and read a magazine. Drawing out her wallet from the bag, she looked up at Natalie. "Be responsible, Nat," she said, handing over a credit card. "You know the back-to-school budget. Try everything on before you buy it, and make sure that you *love* everything you get."

Natalie rolled her eyes good-naturedly. "Oh, I will, Mom . . ." she said. As she and Hannah went out the door, she leaned back in. "Aren't I always responsible?" she asked.

Her mom laughed, and Nat closed the door. She and Hannah headed to the elevators. "I swear," Natalie said, "I've forgotten how to use an elevator—I couldn't remember what floor we lived on when I first got home!"

"But I'm sure you didn't forget about takeout, right?" Hannah teased. "What was the first thing you ordered?"

"Spicy tuna roll . . . mmm . . ." Natalie said, closing her eyes at the memory. "Edamame . . . miso . . . red-bean ice cream . . ."

"Snap out of it, sushi princess," Hannah said. The green light above one of the elevators blinked. "You remember how to get to the lobby?"

Natalie only smiled in response.

In the lobby, Mr. Bartok, one of the regular door-man in Natalie's building, held the door and tipped his hat as the two girls sauntered out to the street. "Good-bye, ladies," he said. Winking at Natalie, he added, "Good to have you back!"

"Thanks, Mr. Bartok," Natalie replied. "Have a great day!" On the sidewalk, she looked at Hannah. "Uptown, or down?"

"Oh, you've been gone longer than I have," Hannah responded, shielding her eyes with her hand and looking up and down the street. "You choose."

"Hannah, you've only been back for a week!"

"I know, but you'd be surprised how much damage I can do in a week."

Natalie laughed. "Good point. Okay, let's just head south. It's gorgeous out—want to walk?"

"Sure," Hannah said. They walked in silence for a few minutes, and Natalie looked up at all the buildings. She had forgotten how *tall* everything was after spending a summer in a place where the highest things around were trees. All around her there were crowds of people pushing and walking and biking and driving. At camp there had been lots of campers, but nothing like this.

Hannah looked over at her. "So I ran into Kyle the other day," she said, breaking the silence. "At the Boathouse in Central Park—he was there with his older brother."

"Really?" Natalie said. "He never wrote to me this summer like he said he was going to."

"Yeah, I know. He told me he left the address at school on the last day and couldn't get anyone to let him in to get it. He looked really miserable about it." Hannah stopped before crossing the street, and looked at Natalie playfully. "Remember how to tell if you can cross?" she teased.

Natalie was quiet for a moment. "So . . . what else did he say about me?"

"Nothing. I told him when you were coming back and that was basically it, because his brother came over and they left."

"Oh." Natalie thought for a minute. "So . . . do you think he's still interested?"

"I don't know, Nat," Hannah said—*almost sharply*, Natalie thought. "Probably."

"Well, the thing is, I met this other guy this summer—you know, I told you about him, Simon—and I really like him—we were basically inseparable. But—"

"Hey," Hannah interrupted, stopping in front of a boutique with cute outfits in the window. "Let's go in here."

"Okay," Natalie said. "So, what do you think—"

"Wow, back-to-school sale!" Hannah said.

Okay, Natalie thought. *She's totally ignoring me—or am I imagining it?* She knew Hannah could be shy, and it might just be weird for her to see Natalie again after so long. She shrugged off the feeling and headed toward the sale racks in the back of the store, where Hannah had already pulled an amazing blue sweater down and was checking the size. "Hannah, that's fantastic," Natalie said, trying to push her worries aside. "You've got to get it!" Hannah slipped the sweater over her head. Even though it didn't match her miniskirt, the sweater looked great on her.

"Yes, you're gorgeous, but does it come in my size?" Natalie asked, and Hannah laughed. It was just like old times. Natalie relaxed and started digging through the rack.

After a few hours of shopping, Natalie's feet started to hurt, and she could definitely sense the beginnings of a killer sunburn. It hadn't occurred to her to put on sunscreen for a day of shopping, but they'd been doing a lot of walking outside, and her shoulders were red and felt warm. "Frappuccino break?" she suggested. They were near the south end of Central Park, and she knew that there was a coffee shop just on the other side of the street. "We could go sit in the park and talk. I feel a serious need to give you the full 411 on Simon!"

"I'm actually kind of hungry," Hannah said. She put down her bags on the sidewalk and reached into her pocket, pulling out her cell phone. "Wow, it's almost six already! I should probably get home."

"I can't believe it's so late!" Natalie replied. "Why don't you come to my place? We'll order in and put aloe on our shoulders. My dad sent me a package of DVDs over the summer that I haven't watched. What do you say? We're way overdue for a gossip session!"

Hannah bit her lip and picked up her shopping bags. "I don't know, Nat. My mom said she wanted me to help with the food shopping, and I promised I wouldn't be gone too long . . ." She trailed off and shifted her weight from one foot to the other. "I'd really better go; I'm going to go catch the subway. I'll see you later, though—Tuesday for sure! Bye!" Without another word, Hannah headed down the street toward the uptown subway station.

"Don't you want to split a cab?" Nat called after her, but Hannah didn't turn around. Natalie walked to the corner and raised her hand to hail a taxi. *Weird*, she thought. *Not like Hannah to pass up movies and takeout.* A yellow cab pulled up next to her and she got in. *Whatever. She's probably just tired*, she decided. "I'm going to Seventy-ninth and West End," she told the cab driver. The meter clicked on, and she sat back against the cool, smooth seats, enjoying the air-conditioning. It was good to be back in New York—but it was strange; she had thought seeing Hannah would be more fun.

I'm being crazy, she decided. *All that fresh air went to my brain. It's the only explanation. Right?*

Jenna> SATURDAY

Jenna looked over at her brother, who was lying on the couch in their dad's basement, reading some new comic that he had brought along for the weekend. She sighed loudly, and when he didn't look up or comment, she sighed again, louder this time. Finally, Adam looked up. "What's wrong with you?" he asked, sounding annoyed.

"I'm so bored, Ad," Jenna replied, hoping her voice sounded as pitiful as she felt. She could not believe that she was stuck at her dad's new place on her first Saturday night back from camp—in a town where she didn't know anyone but her two brothers and her sister, and where there was absolutely nothing to do.

The night before hadn't been bad; it had been two months since the four kids had been all together, and it was great to see their dad. They had stayed up really late (later than their mom ever would have let them) and watched talk shows and the late movie and told their dad all about camp. And then they'd slept in the next morning, which had been great after getting up at the crack of dawn all summer. But then as Saturday had rolled on, Jenna found herself wanting to die from boredom.

"Why don't you watch TV?" Adam suggested. He rolled over onto his stomach and looked back down at his comic book.

Jenna sighed for a third time. "Adam, you know Dad doesn't have the cable hooked up yet."

"So? Watch network," Adam said. "You've been at camp. Just pretend you're still roughing it."

"It's Saturday night!" Jenna cried. "There's nothing *on* network. *Nothing*. Maybe, like, some Hallmark Hall of Fame movie. Anyway, I don't feel like watching TV. We've been staring at that screen all day." She knew she had a point there. After breakfast, their dad had insisted on taking them to Blockbuster, where they'd rented more movies than they could ever watch in a weekend. Even a weekend in a boring town where they didn't know anyone and where there wasn't anything to do.

The five of them had watched one movie, but then

Steph and Matt had escaped to the mall, and Dad had gone upstairs to do some more unpacking and decorating.

That had been seven hours ago. Jenna and Adam hadn't left the basement since. They'd watched another movie, checked out every single website they knew, and finally, Adam had retreated to the couch with his comic book. At around one, their dad had brought down a piping hot pizza he'd ordered, plus a two-liter bottle of soda. They weren't in the mood for pizza because their mom had taken them out for pizza the night before, but they didn't want to hurt their dad's feelings. So they ate and talked for half an hour or so, and then interminable boredom had set in when their dad went upstairs to clean. Three hours later, they had completely run out of things to do.

Just thinking about how bored she was made Jenna feel worse. "Adddaaaaam," Jenna whined. "Can't we, like, play cards or something?"

Adam looked over his comic at her. "If Dad has cards, they're not unpacked," he said. "We've ransacked this place. Come on, just check your e-mail or something."

"I already did. When did Steph and Matt say they were coming home? Maybe they'll take us out."

Adam snorted. "To where, pizza and a movie?"

Jenna flopped onto the floor. "And I'm supposed to be the joker," she said. She sighed. "Even just driving around would be better than this."

Just then, a car pulled up. Jumping up and clapping her hands together, Jenna shouted, "Thank God! They're back!" Adam didn't respond but just rolled back over onto his back.

Jenna ran up the stairs two at a time. "Steph! Matt!" she called excitedly. "Do you guys want to—" When she reached the living room, she stopped. The door was wide open, but looming inside the entrance was a guy who was definitely not one of her siblings. It was a delivery guy, with a bag overflowing with Chinese takeout in one hand and a two-liter bottle of soda in a plastic bag in the other.

"Look, Jen!" her dad said, beaming. "I ordered us takeout!" He handed some folded cash to the delivery guy, who shoved the money in his pocket, turned, and left. Jenna's dad swung the door closed and carried the food into the kitchen. Jenna followed and sank into a kitchen chair while her dad opened cabinets, taking down plates and glasses.

"And," her dad said, looking excited, "open up the freezer! There's a surprise in there, too!"

Jenna sighed and got up. When she opened the freezer, she gasped—it was absolutely chock-full of tons of different flavors of ice cream! Her dad laughed out loud. "I figured you probably didn't get much ice cream at camp," he said. "So I thought I'd make up for it."

"Wow, Dad," Jenna said slowly. "You certainly did." She sat back down at the table. "But . . . I mean, we did have takeout for lunch," she went on. "And we went out for dinner last night. Mom took us." Her dad put the plates down on the table, and then slipped into a chair, looking dejected. She could tell she'd hurt her dad's feelings, even though she hadn't meant to. "But this smells delicious," Jenna said quickly, trying to make him feel better. She opened a box and dumped a pile of lo mein onto her plate, then picked up chopsticks and dug in. "Seriously, it's great," she said, slurping up a noodle.

Her dad looked up hopefully. "I was thinking after dinner, we could get out the Scrabble board and play," he said. "You and me, and Adam if he wants to. What do you say?"

"That sounds great," Jenna responded, thinking, *Anything's better than another movie.*

Her dad reached out and fluffed her hair. "Great, kiddo," he said. "Why don't you run and get Adam for dinner?"

On her way down to the basement, Jenna heard a car pulling into the driveway. "Are they back?" Adam called up to her, hearing her footsteps on the stairs.

"I think so," Jenna said, walking over to sit next to him. "Listen, Ad . . . we're having takeout for dinner again. That car we heard before was the delivery guy."

Adam looked at her in disbelief. "Are you kidding me?" he said, putting down his comic book. "That's like, three meals in a row. I thought Dad would maybe grill hamburgers or something."

"Yeah, I know," Jenna said. She rolled her eyes. "He's like, trying to be Superdad. How much do you want to bet he tries to take us to the zoo or something tomorrow?"

"Seriously," her brother said, sitting up. "On the other hand, though, Mom hardly ever lets us eat restaurant food every night. Maybe this'll be nice—kind of break up the monotony of Mom's chicken and rice, chicken and noodles, chicken and potatoes . . ." Jenna laughed. "Chicken with asparagus . . ." Adam went on.

Jenna picked up a couch pillow and whacked him with it. "Come on, loser," she said. "Let's go eat. And then I'll kick your butt at Scrabble."

"I can hardly wait," Adam said dryly. He got up off

the couch and Jenna followed him upstairs to the kitchen, where Steph and Matt were regaling their dad with tales from their long day at the mall.

Looking at the Chinese takeout boxes, Jenna suddenly had no appetite. "I think I'm gonna go to bed, Dad," she said.

"Why, peanut?" he asked, looking concerned. "You feeling okay?"

"Yeah, I'm just tired," she said. "Long day, and all." She walked out of the room.

"What about Scrabble?" her dad called after her. She stopped and turned back to him.

"Maybe tomorrow?" she said. "I'm really tired."

Her dad got up and crossed the kitchen to where she stood, her arms crossed over her chest. "Really, Jen, are you feeling all right?" he asked.

"Seriously, Dad, I'm fine," she snapped.

"Okay," he replied. "But if anything's wrong . . ."

"Nothing's wrong. I just want to go to bed." She walked away, even though she could tell her dad was still standing there.

In the bedroom that she was sharing with Steph, she lay down on her bed. After a few minutes, Steph walked in. "What's up with you?" her sister asked accusingly.

"Nothing," Jenna replied. "I'm just tired."

"Look, Jen, I'm sure you had a boring day today. And don't think it's escaped me that this is the third meal of takeout we've had in the last two days. But don't be so hard on Dad. He's having a rough time right now."

"Aren't you bored too, Steph?" Jenna asked, sitting up on the bed.

"Yes. I totally am. Do you know what I did today?"

"No," Jenna admitted. She looked up at her sister. "What did you do?"

"I went to the mall with Matt, who just wanted to ditch me and go hang out at the Discovery store or something. So I went to Barnes and Noble and read magazines. Like *all* the magazines. I was starting on *Outdoor Living* when Matt finally came and asked if we could go home."

"Oh," Jenna said. "I guess it was a pretty blah day for everyone."

"Yeah, it was. Now, can you come eat dinner and play Scrabble with us?" Steph said, crossing her arms and tapping her foot impatiently. "Seriously. Dad really wants to."

Jenna got up. "Yeah, all right," she said.

The two girls walked to the living room, where Adam had set up a card table and was placing chairs around it. Their dad walked out of the kitchen with a huge bowl of popcorn. Catching Jenna's eye, he smiled. "Nobody wanted dinner," he said. "Guess we just have to eat ice cream and popcorn."

Jenna smiled. She had to admit, that didn't sound too bad.

SUNDAY

In the morning, Jenna woke up before her sister and brothers and wandered out to the kitchen. She was hoping to catch her dad alone to ask him if they could go back home a little earlier than planned, just so she could meet up with friends or get some shopping done before school started. She wanted to get things ready for school after being away all summer.

But she stopped short in the doorway: Her dad was sitting at the table, but he had his head in his hands and his shoulders were shaking. At first, Jenna thought he was laughing—but then she realized that her dad was crying. She tried to back quietly away, but he looked up suddenly.

"Jenna! Good morning, sunshine!" he said, trying to act like nothing was wrong and quickly brushing a stray tear from his face.

"Morning, Dad," Jenna said. She moved tentatively into the kitchen.

"Eggs? Toast? Sausage? Bacon? Porridge? Oatmeal?" her dad asked jovially, getting up from his chair and moving over to the fridge. As he poked his head in, she saw him again wipe at his eyes.

"Toast would be great," she said.

"Great," her dad said. "But you'd better have some eggs, too—I've got a big day planned for us. The zoo! Bowling! And I was going to take you guys out for pizza, but now I'm thinking maybe this cool sandwich place where I ate on the day I moved in. They make a BLT that's six layers high!"

"Yum," Jenna said halfheartedly. She smiled. "That sounds delicious, Dad."

"Or we could save that place for next weekend, and go for sushi instead . . ." Her dad pulled a carton of eggs out of the fridge, closed the door, and reached onto the top of the fridge for a loaf of bread. "Whaddya think? Sounds like a great day, right?"

Jenna barely heard him. Looking at the expression on her dad's face, she felt guilty for wanting to go home early, even though she did have a lot to do—he looked so excited at his idea of the perfect day. But . . .

"Right, Dad," she said. "Great."

"This is gonna be great, Jenna," he replied. Jenna could tell he really wanted it to be, but she had a terrible feeling that not only was her parents' divorce splitting up their family, it was going to make middle school even harder to get used to.

"Right. Great." Jenna sighed. She only hoped it was the truth.

⛺ ⛺ ⛺

To: Aries8
From: NatalieNYC
Subject: happy sunday!

hey, jenna! just wanted to write you a quick note—— sorry i had to go without talking much yesterday, but my best friend, hannah, showed up and we had plans to go shopping. i bought so much fabulous stuff! it's so great being back in the city and being able to see my friends from home. i totally miss all of you guys, though!

are you SO relieved to be home? i mean, i just got back into the normal swing of things. i can't believe i'm admitting this, but i'm actually kind of looking forward to next summer . . . but for the next 10 months, it's sushi, frappuccinos, and shopping for me!

hope everything is going well. have a great time, and tell me how school goes once you start!

xoxo, natalie

chapter TWO

grace> MONDAY

Posted by: Brynn
Subject: Good morning, campers!

Can you believe school is about to start already? We've only been home for a few days, barely any time to relax, and all of a sudden we have to start getting up early again! I've really loved being able to sleep in again, though . . . and watch TV, and go shopping . . .

But I am excited to go back to school. It's going to be so cool this year! At my school, the sixth-graders aren't at middle school—they're still at the elementary school, and next year we go to the junior high school. So this year, we rule! I can't wait.

Hey, Grace, are you going to join drama club? You have to! You were the best actress at camp by far (and you know it's hard for me to admit that!).

My mom is calling—we have a Labor Day barbecue thing, so I better go. Happy Labor Day, everybody, and have a great first day tomorrow! Love, Brynn

Grace sat patiently as her mom slid two strips of bacon next to the steaming-hot eggs already on the plate in front of her. Across the table, her dad was doing the crossword puzzle in the newspaper and sipping a cup of coffee. "Grace," he said, poking his head over the paper, "what's a five-letter word for 'mad,' first letter L?"

Grace thought for a minute. "I have no idea, Dad, sorry," she said. She made a funny little "angry" face and shook her fists, but of course, that was no help. Her dad sighed and went back to the paper.

"Livid," her mom said, sitting down next to Grace with a plate of food for herself. "Need juice, Gracie?"

"I'll get it," Grace said. She got up and opened the refrigerator.

"So, Grace," her father said, folding up his newspaper and looking at her with a serious expression. "How's your reading coming?"

Grace pulled the carton of orange juice out from behind a stack of Tupperware and sat back down at the table. "Great!" she said. "I finished my last book last night. *Bridge to Terabithia*. It was really good. It's about this girl who—"

"That's wonderful, honey," her mom interrupted her. "I'm very proud of how hard you've worked this summer. You'll be perfectly ready to get back to school."

"Definitely," Grace agreed. "I am so excited. My friend Brynn posted on our camp blog this morning asking if I was going to join drama club, and I'm signing up first thing tomorrow! I can't wait! Especially since Emily is going to be at a different middle school—this will be a good way for me to . . ." She stopped when she noticed her parents exchanging one of their famous looks. Her face darkened. They knew she was nervous about making all new friends now that her BFF was zoned to a different school district! "What?" she asked, suddenly worried.

Her mom sighed. "Well, we've been meaning to talk to you about this, Grace. Your dad and I don't think it's a good idea for you to join the drama club this year."

Grace put down her glass. "What? Why not?" she asked.

"Your mother and I think you need to focus on getting your grades up," her dad responded. "You did a great job this summer with your reading, but you have to prove that you can continue working hard."

"But Dad, I *will* keep working hard, I swear!" Grace promised. She could feel her face starting to turn red—a sure sign she was about to cry. "You saw how well I did this summer—I can keep working hard *and* join the drama club!"

Grace's father shook his head. "Grace, I'm sorry. I'm not going to back down on this one."

Grace looked at her mom. "Mom? Please?"

"No, honey, I'm sorry. Your dad and I discussed this already; we decided that you wouldn't be allowed to join any extracurricular activities until we see real evidence that your grades are going up. I'm very sorry, and I am very proud of how well you've done so far and we know you can keep it up. You can join the club next year."

Grace couldn't believe they wouldn't let her join the club. Over the summer, she had realized how much she loved to act—she loved being onstage, with people watching her while she performed. It was an amazing rush. A tear slipped down her cheek, and she shoved her plate away and stood up so fast that her chair fell over.

"I can't believe this!" she exclaimed. Her chin began to tremble, and she had to run away before she completely broke down into tears. As she ran up the stairs, she really started to cry.

Grace threw herself onto her bed and sobbed with her face in a pillow. *This stinks*, she thought. *This totally stinks*. She rolled over, with tears still streaming down her cheeks, and sat up. Doing so, she caught a glimpse of her summer reading books, stacked neatly on her desk next to her computer.

She got up and crossed her room, sliding into the chair at her desk. She logged on to Instant Messenger, but none of her friends were online. *Great*, she thought. *No friends, no drama club* . . . Before the tears could slide out again, she opened up her Web browser and tried to distract herself. She knew she should respond to Brynn's question about drama club, but she was mortified that her parents weren't going to let her—and all because of her grades. Plus, Brynn had sounded excited about school starting, and Grace was decidedly not.

However, Julie, the counselor she'd had at camp, had set a blog up for all the bunkmates to keep in touch when they got back home, and Grace was interested in what was going on in everyone's lives. She opened the site and found three new messages. One was a welcome note from Julie, which included Julie's e-mail address, phone number, and mailing address. There was another message from Marissa, the counselor-in-training from their bunk, but Grace was the most excited about the message from her friend Alex.

Dear Other Campers, the letter began. Grace smiled. Typical of Alex to be so formal about something so friendly.

I hope everybody's having a great time back at home! I know you are all missing getting up at the crack of dawn, smelling funny, and eating terrible, disgusting, horrible food. I am too. Anyway, I just wanted to write to tell you all that I miss you so much . . . and I hope we can get together soon! Let's keep in touch here as much as possible—I want to hear about everyone's sixth-grade experience!

Love,

Alex

Grace sighed. She was sure that other people *were* glad to be back with their friends—and she was, too—but she really wasn't looking forward to her sixth-grade experience anymore. So far, it just seemed like it wasn't going to be fun. She logged off of the computer without writing a response.

On the desk, next to her stack of books, was a picture from camp that Grace had framed when she got home. It was the cast from the camp play. She picked up the frame and looked closely at the picture. *I look so happy*, she thought. *I guess part of it is that I thought I'd be able to keep acting.* She sighed and put down the photograph.

Then a thought crossed her mind. She knew her parents wouldn't be home from work until five thirty each night, and this year they'd decided she was too old for a babysitter. They'd given her a key and everything.

And drama club was after school every day from three to five.

So . . . Her mind was whirling. With no parents or babysitter home after school, no one would know what time she came home. And if she came home right away after drama, they would just assume she'd been there since three! *It's the perfect plan,* she thought excitedly.

Nervous butterflies hit her stomach. It was risky, even though it seemed like it could work. It was just a matter of pulling it off. She decided she'd calm down, act totally mature through the barbecue, and then ask about drama club again.

And if they said no? Well, then Grace was just going to have to take matters into her own hands.

"Grace," her mother called. "Let's get going—it looks like rain, and I'd like to get to your grandma's before it starts pouring."

"Coming," Grace yelled. She pulled on a light hoodie and stepped into her new sandals—well, not *new* new. She'd bought them before camp, but hadn't brought them along because she didn't want to risk them being ruined. They were leather, with awesome purple beading on the straps. She was sure they'd be a hit at the barbecue.

She ran down the stairs, where her parents were waiting by the door. "Grace, honey, don't you think you ought to change your shoes?" her mom asked. "They're leather, and if it rains . . ." She trailed off before describing the unspeakable horror of Grace's leather shoes getting wet in the rain. "Why don't you wear your sneakers?"

In that instant, Grace's bad mood sparked back, but she held her tongue. "Good thinking, Mom," she said, smiling sweetly. She changed into her sneakers and followed her parents out the door.

It did start to rain the second they reached Grace's grandma's house. The barbecue was low-key, just family sitting around Grandma's living room eating hamburgers off paper plates. Grace thought she did a pretty good job of acting grown-up and mature, so as they were leaving, after she buckled herself up in the backseat of her dad's green sedan, she leaned forward and tapped her mom on the shoulder.

"So, about drama club," she said sweetly, figuring it was worth one more shot.

"No, Grace," her mother said impatiently.

"I'm just wondering if we could work out a deal," Grace continued quickly. "Like if I can keep a B average, then I get to stay in it."

Grace's mother twisted around in her seat. "No, honey. If you get a B average we'll talk about you joining next year."

"But at camp . . ." Grace began to counter.

"Camp was different," Grace's father jumped in. "Camp was a couple of books, and lots of time to read. And lots of girls helping you. Camp was different than middle school. And you need to learn that, honey. I'm sorry. But the topic is closed." To illustrate his point, he reached over and turned on the radio. A man's boring voice droned out of the speakers, and Grace leaned back against the slightly sticky leather of the hot backseat.

"Can you turn on the air-conditioning?" she said, feeling defeated. For a moment, she'd really believed that her parents would have changed their minds while she was upstairs in her room. But she was wrong. Grace wasn't the kind of girl who normally went against what her parents asked of her. But desperate times called for desperate measures, didn't they?

Good thing I have a backup plan, she thought to herself.

To: BrynnWins
From: Grrrrace
Subject: Back to School!

Hey, Brynn!
Are you amped to start school tomorrow? I hope you have a great time ruling the school! I'll be jealous while I'm trying to figure out where all my classes are.
Sorry this is so short——I've got to get to bed!
Luv,
Grace

Alex> TUESDAY

BEEP
BEEP
BEEP

Alex groaned and rolled over to swat her alarm clock. "Six thirty already?" she moaned. It was the first day of school and she was already ready for summer vacation to swing around again.

Pulling herself out of bed, she stumbled out the door and down the hall to the bathroom. After a nice hot shower, maybe she'd start to feel like herself again.

After her shower, she pulled on the outfit she'd decided on the night before: her favorite jeans and a cool yellow shirt she'd gotten at the mall over the weekend. She blow-dried and brushed her long black hair and pulled it back into a ponytail, and as a finishing touch, put on a pair of white socks with little frogs on them and her favorite green sneakers. Appraising herself in the full-length mirror that hung in the hallway, she thought to herself, *Perfect!* Casual, cute, and not too girly. She was ready to face school.

Downstairs, her mother had poured a bowl of Cheerios for her and set it on the table with a glass of orange juice. "Eat up, Alex," her mom said. "Excited about school?"

"Yeah!" Alex replied, sitting down and taking a big gulp of juice. "Totally. I got an e-mail yesterday about soccer tryouts, too—they are today after school. So I won't be home till five."

Alex's mother put down the newspaper she was reading. "That's very exciting, honey," she said. "Do you know anyone else who's trying out?"

"Well, I think a lot of the girls from my team last year will try out," Alex said. Just then, Alex's father walked into the kitchen, jangling his keys.

"Ready to go, Al?" he said. He leaned over and kissed Alex's mom, and then looked at Alex expectantly. "We'd better get a move on if you're going to be at school on time."

"Can't be late on the first day!" Alex's mom said. She got up and walked over to Alex. "Take a few more bites, and then you should get going!"

Alex shoveled a few more spoonfuls of cereal into her mouth, and then stood up to kiss her mom good-bye. She grabbed her brand-new backpack from the floor, where she'd placed it the previous day, and shifted it onto her shoulders. "Ready!"

The drive to school didn't take long. Alex's dad gave her a few dollars for lunch, and she ran excitedly into the school lobby. Instantly, though, as she entered the crowded room, she knew she was more worried than she had let on. There were so many people packed in—and they were all so *old*! She felt like a baby—all the other kids were taller and bigger than she was. The boys looked like grown men, and the girls looked like adult women. Some of the boys even had *mustaches*! And the girls . . . well, they were obviously not in elementary school anymore.

In the corners of the lobby, Alex could see small groups of what had to be sixth-graders, all huddled together, looking young and scared. She stood stock-still and scanned the room, looking for a familiar face. Finally, she saw one across the room—her best friend, Bridgette. Their eyes met, and obvious relief crossed both of their faces. *Thank God*, Alex thought. Bridgette was wearing one of her typical anime-logo T-shirts. At least *some* things never changed. She scurried over to her friend.

"Hi!" Bridgette squealed, throwing her arms around Alex for a big hug.

Alex was about to launch into a long tale about her exploits at Camp Lakeview when a loud voice boomed over the loudspeaker. "ALL STUDENTS TO THE GYMNASIUM," the man's deep voice said. "ALL STUDENTS TO THE GYMNASIUM FOR WELCOME ASSEMBLY." Bridgette and Alex looked at each other.

"Well, here we go," Alex said nervously.

Bridgette laughed. "Oh, come on, Alex. It'll be fun!" She looped her arm through her friend's and propelled them both toward the gym, where the other students were beginning to gather. They made their way through the packed room and found seats on the end of the bleachers farthest from the door. Looking around the room, Alex was surprised that the school's cheerleaders had already started to work. The walls were plastered with GO, ROCKETS! LAUNCH! THREE, TWO, ONE, BLAST-OFF! and other signs supporting the football, volleyball, and soccer teams. She was about to lean over to Bridgette and ask when the cheerleaders had started practice when the principal, Mr. Delaney, walked to a podium in the middle of the gym floor and began to speak.

"Welcome back, everyone," his voice droned. "We hope you had a fun, safe, and educational summer."

At this, some of the older boys laughed, and a boy behind Alex said to one of his friends, "Well . . . fun, any-way!"

"There are a couple of reminders: First, tryouts for the girls' soccer team are tonight, on the main field, at 3 PM. Those who make it past cuts will meet tomorrow after school. . . ."

He went on talking, but Alex had stopped listening. *First tryouts?* she thought frantically. She hadn't heard anything about there being cuts . . . Suddenly, she was very, very nervous. She tuned back in to the assembly just in time to hear Mr. Delaney finish talking. ". . . And good luck to all of you. We are glad to have you back," he said half-heartedly. "Please go to homeroom, where you will receive your schedules and locker assignments."

Luckily, Alex knew where her homeroom was. During the previous year, her class had come to the middle school to take a tour and learn the way around. She and Bridgette stood up and headed in the direction of the science wing, where their rooms were. Because Bridgette's last name was in the end of the alphabet, she'd been placed into a different room, but Alex figured she'd still have some classes with her friend. She also had expected to know at least a few kids in her homeroom. But she didn't—everyone was either older or from a different elementary school. She sat down near the front of the classroom and smiled tentatively at the girl sitting next to her, but the girl just looked at her and then looked away.

Her teacher took roll and passed out the schedules and locker assignments, and before Alex even had time to try to remember anyone's name, the period was over and they were all thrust back into the crowded hallway.

As Alex walked down the hall toward her locker, she studied her schedule. It looked okay—basic stuff, like American history, geography, intro to algebra, a PE class, a study hall, and English. *I can totally handle this*, she thought. In fact, she was even sort of excited about American history, which she had first period.

At her locker (once she finally figured out how to open the combination lock) she made sure she had her new notebook and a bright red pen in her backpack. She slammed her locker shut and headed for American history, shoving her way through the hallway and praying no one would trip her—accidentally or otherwise.

She made it to class with seconds to spare, and breathlessly slid into the only open seat, which was right in the middle of the front row. As she pulled her notebook out of her bag and opened it to the first page, the girl next to her leaned over. "Hey, Alex!" the brown-haired girl whispered.

Shocked, Alex looked over. "Lucy!" she exclaimed. "Hi!" She and Lucy had known each other in elementary school, but not well. Still, Alex was glad to see any familiar face.

Their teacher walked into the room and closed the door behind him. "Good morning, class," he said. "I trust that your summers were productive." Alex heard some snickers from the back of the room, where she had seen some older boys sitting. "My name is Mr. Garfield, and I will be guiding you through a historical tour of the United States in the seventeenth, eighteenth, and nineteenth centuries. Girls," he said, motioning to Alex and Lucy, "would you mind helping me pass out our guidebooks?" He pointed at a huge stack of American history textbooks sitting on a table in the front of the room. Alex could feel her face turning red. She looked over at Lucy, who shrugged, and they got up and passed out the textbooks, being careful to not look anyone in the eye.

The rest of the morning passed uneventfully. Alex perfected running to her locker as soon as the bell rang at the end of class; once at her locker she'd cram whatever she needed into her bag. At lunchtime, she was overjoyed to see Bridgette and compare schedules; it turned out they had a math class together at the end of the day, and Alex spent most of the afternoon looking forward to seeing her friend.

It was weird, though. When they arrived in their seventh-period math class, Bridgette already had a small group of friends with her. She saw Alex come in and motioned her over to a nearby empty seat. "Hey, Al!" she said. "This is Vanessa and Mary-Ann."

"Hey," Alex said.

"We have, like, all our classes together!" Bridgette said excitedly. "How's your day going?"

"Okay," Alex replied. "This girl Lucy is in my history class first period, which is cool."

"That's good," Bridgette said, smiling. She turned

to Vanessa. "So, do you think he has a girlfriend?" she asked, picking up the conversation the girls had been having before Alex arrived.

Since Alex didn't really know whom it was they were talking about, all she could do was sit quietly and hope she'd catch on soon enough. It was a long forty minutes.

▲ ▲ ▲

After class, Bridgette gave Alex a quick hug and said, "Good luck in tryouts!" before she scurried away with Vanessa. Alex slowly walked to her locker to get her gym bag.

On the way to the locker room to change into her soccer clothes, Alex passed the computer lab and decided to go in. The big room was filled with dozens of computers, most of them already being used by kids trying to get a jump on their newly assigned homework. Alex slid into a chair and logged on. She quickly checked her e-mail and then accessed the blog set up by her bunk in order to keep track of everyone. There weren't many entries yet—she figured everyone was busy getting back into the swing of things.

She glanced up at the clock over the door of the lab, and realized she only had about twenty minutes before she had to be ready and on the field. Sighing, she clicked on "Compose New Entry" and slid deeper into her seat. She had a sinking feeling that the tryouts were going to be worse than expected.

Posted by: Alex
Title: Soccer worries . . .

Hey, guys! Sorry to have my first-day-of-school blog entry be kind of a downer, but I wanted to vent a little. I'm supernervous about soccer tryouts—and they start in 20 minutes! I've never had to try out for a soccer team before, and I'm worried about all the older girls. I know I'm not going to be the star like I was in fifth grade. Any of you guys having experiences like this? Middle school's like a whole different world! Anyway, I better go get dressed. Keep in touch, everybody, and I hope you're all having a great time!
Love,
Alex

Before she could log off, Alex noticed that someone had already left a reply to her entry. She clicked on the line that read One Reply.

Posted by: Brynn
Re: Soccer worries . . .

A! You're a great soccer player! No worries—you will be GREAT. Love you and miss you xo! Brynn

Feeling slightly better, Alex logged off from the computer and stood up, buoyed by her friend's faith in her. She left the computer lab and headed down to the locker room, with butterflies in her tummy, but getting excited to play soccer again.

Posted by: Natalie
Subject: first day over!

hey, everyone. so, i just got out of my first day of school. it was pretty good—a lot of the kids were in my elementary school. i saw kyle . . . he looked supercute in a brown button-down and jeans. besides that, not much to report. i'm exhausted, though! all that running between classes! i'm going to ask my mom if we can go out to dinner to celebrate the first day of sixth grade.

luv you all,
nat

chapter

THREE

grace> FRIDAY

"No, my favorite is definitely *Romeo and Juliet*," Lara said. She picked up her can of apple juice and took a long sip. "I mean, *Macbeth* is cool—"

"You're not supposed to call it that," Greg interrupted her. "You're supposed to call it *The Scottish Play*."

"Isn't that only when you're like, performing it?" another boy, Andrew, jumped in. "I think you can call it *Macbeth* when you're not." He reached over and took a few of Greg's potato chips.

Grace put down her bag of baby carrots. "What do you mean? Why can't you call it *Macbeth*?" Her drama club friends knew the weirdest things about theater stuff.

"It's bad luck, or something," Andrew said, shrugging his shoulders. "I don't think it really matters if Lara calls it that when we're working on scenes from *My Fair Lady*."

"You're probably right," Greg said. "But I wouldn't take any chances."

Lara and Grace looked at each other and laughed. The four kids were seated cross-legged in a circle in their school's huge theater, sharing snacks during their ten-minute break at drama club. It was only halfway through the club's first meeting, but Grace had already become great friends with Lara, Andrew, and Greg. She even had plans to go to a movie with Lara over the weekend. She'd barely had time to feel guilty about lying to her parents, though she realized she'd have to do some damage control and tell Lara to just say she was Grace's friend from class.

"Anyway, since I was so *rudely* interrupted," Lara said teasingly, "like I was saying, *Romeo and Juliet* is my favorite. I just love Shakespeare. He's so *romantic*."

"Yeah," Andrew said, rolling his eyes. "It's so sweet how they die at the end." He and Greg burst out laughing.

"Whatever," Lara replied, pushing a strand of her long brown hair behind her ear. "All I know is, it's romantic, and beautiful, and like, the best love story ever." "I know," Grace said excitedly. "When Leonardo DiCaprio finds Claire Danes lying on that—" She stopped abruptly, noticing Lara's sly smile. "What?"

"It's way more romantic in the actual *play*, Grace," Lara said, grinning.

"Oh," Grace responded, feeling slightly stupid. "I haven't read it."

"Really?" Lara asked nonchalantly. "We read it last year in my English class—"

"Wow, really?" Grace said. "Isn't it pretty hard?" She knew that Shakespeare's plays were usually read during middle school or high school—she couldn't imagine someone reading it during a class in elementary school.

Lara shrugged. "Come on," she said. "I mean, it is in *English*," she joked, reaching over to squeeze Grace's arm affectionately.

Grace looked down at the floor. "Yeah, I know," she said. "I mean, obviously it is."

Andrew laughed. "Whatever, Lara, we didn't all go to smarty-pants school for fifth grade." Grace relaxed a bit, remembering that Lara had gone to a super-exclusive private school, but had decided to stick to public school for sixth grade because there wasn't a good drama club at the private middle school.

"Speaking of smarty pants," Greg said, "can you guys believe the homework we have already?" He leaned over and grabbed one of Grace's baby carrots and shoved it into his mouth.

"I know," Grace said. Even on the first day of school she'd spent two hours doing homework, and the load had gotten considerably worse since. "I've had tons of homework every single night." She took a deep breath and looked around at her new friends. "The worst part is," she admitted, "my parents think I'm staying at the library after school instead of coming to drama club, so I have to hole up in my room and pretend like I'm on the Internet or something, or they'll get suspicious."

"How come they won't let you be in drama club, anyway?" Greg asked.

Grace sighed. "It's complicated," she replied. She didn't want to get into the problems she'd had in school the previous year. "They just want me to spend more time on my schoolwork, I guess."

"It's too bad that you have to lie to them," Andrew said.

Grace sighed again. "Yeah, I know." She flung the back of her head against her forehead dramatically to lighten the moment. "Anyway," she said, changing the subject, "what kind of homework do you guys have for the weekend?"

"Where do I begin?" Greg joked. He leaned back and began ticking the work off on his fingers. "Two pages of math problems, a North American geography work sheet, plus there's a quiz in my world history class on Monday that I totally have to study for. Can you believe there's a quiz already?"

"That's rough," Andrew said sympathetically. "I only have to read the second chapter of *Animal Farm*. Shouldn't be too bad."

Greg moaned. "Oh, man . . . I have that too!"

"Me too," Lara said, picking up one of Grace's carrots and twirling it around in her fingers like a miniature baton. "Plus math. I'm going to try to get it done tonight, though—I hate doing work on the weekends!"

"Wow," Grace said jealously. "You guys are all in the same English class? I don't know anybody in my classes yet, except a couple of people who went to Washington Elementary with me."

Greg and Andrew looked at each other. "No . . ." Lara said. "Aren't you reading *Animal Farm* too? I thought it was a sixth-grade requirement or something."

"Oh," Grace said. "Um, no, my class isn't reading it. We're reading *Hatchet* right now."

"I read that last year," Greg said casually.

"Well, I didn't," Grace snapped. Seeing the hurt look on Greg's face, she immediately felt bad. "But we went to different schools," she added in a softer voice.

"Yeah," Lara said. "We've probably read tons of different books." She threw a strange, confused look at Grace. "Anyway, so, what homework do you have, Grace, besides *Hatchet?*"

Grace took a deep breath. "Um . . . *Hatchet*, and a couple of pages of math," she said. "I guess it isn't that bad. It's way more than in fifth grade, though." She picked up a carrot and put it in her mouth, but she wasn't hungry anymore. She just felt sad.

"Tell me about it," Greg moaned. "Fifth grade was a *breeze* compared to this."

"Not as fun, though," Andrew said. "This year's off to a great start!"

"Totally," Lara replied. She smiled reassuringly at Grace. "I bet we'll all get the hang of it before we know it though, right, Grace?"

"I hope so!" Grace said, smiling back at her new friend.

"Okay, kids, let's regroup," Mrs. West, the drama club leader said from her perch onstage. "Let's try it from Eliza's entrance . . . and this time, Grace, will you please play Eliza, and Andrew, Mr. Higgins?"

Grace scrambled to her feet, snatching up the carrots as she stood. After shoving the baggie into her backpack, she marched to the stage and climbed the few stairs on stage left. "What page are we on?" she asked Mrs. West.

▲   ▲   ▲

Later, walking home, Grace tried to figure out why *Animal Farm* was such a touchy subject for her. She knew she was smart; she just had trouble reading. But it hurt to know that her friends were all doing just fine, while she was struggling to read a book that Greg had finished in fifth grade.

It *was* hard. To Grace, reading anything was hard. It took a lot of concentration and effort to even get through a few pages. For the past few nights, she'd been staying up far past her bedtime, curled under her blanket with a flashlight and her copy of *Hatchet*, and she was already a little behind in class. She sighed, and kicked a pebble on the sidewalk in front of her. "Sometimes I'm so *stupid*," she said aloud.

But she knew she wasn't stupid. She just had a hard time concentrating on reading, that was all. Still, she knew it was going to take a lot more late nights to finish *Hatchet*. And there was bound to be way more homework in her future. For the first time she almost regretted her decision to join the drama club. Almost.

Grace scurried up the stairs to her room, threw her backpack on the ground, and turned on her computer. She immediately went to her camp's blog. Alex's entry about soccer tryouts on Tuesday had sparked a long conversation that included almost all of the girls—everyone, in fact, except for Chelsea, had left encouraging messages for Alex.

Grace knew that her camp friends would understand what she was going through. After all, when they'd found out about her summer reading, they had formed a book club to help. But even after she read through all of their entries and responses to one another, she logged off and turned the computer off without writing a word.

Picking her backpack up off the floor, she dug through the papers and books inside, finally drawing out her copy of *Hatchet*. She sighed, crawled into her bed, and opened to the page that she'd bookmarked that day in study hall. She was on page thirteen.

An hour later, when she heard the front door slam and her dad's footsteps on the stairs, she was only on page twenty. Her dad poked his head into her room without knocking and Grace put her finger in the book to keep her place. "Hi, honey," he said. "How was school?"

"Pretty good," Grace said.

"Did you go to the library afterward? I called here a couple of hours ago to see if you wanted me to pick up anything for you at Chung's Chinese, but there wasn't an answer."

"Yeah, I'm working on this book," Grace said, holding up *Hatchet* for her dad to see.

Her father walked farther into the room and took the book from her, putting his own finger in where Grace's had been. "Wow, *Hatchet*, huh?" he said. "Looks like one I'd like."

"It is, Dad," Grace said. "It's about this boy who gets stranded in the wilderness."

"Sounds great, Grace." He handed the book back to her. "Why don't you take a break and come down for dinner? I got you some sweet-and-sour chicken. Figured that would be okay."

"Thanks, Dad," Grace said. "But I'm not hungry right now. Is it okay if I come and eat later?"

"Of course, sweetie," he said. "Enjoy your book!" He turned and left the room, shutting the door behind him. And Grace, who was starving, went back to her reading, determined to get through another couple of pages before going downstairs to her Chinese food.

natalie > FRIDAY

Posted by: Natalie
Subject: school social TONIGHT!

hey, everyone! this will be a short posting because I have to get ready to go to our back-to-school social and hannah's coming by in about half an hour (barely enough time for me to get dressed!). i'm so excited—i've never been to a dance like this before. i'm wearing a brand-new outfit! an awesome denim mini and a really cute pink top that has little rhinestones on it, plus some new boots. anyway, just wanted to tell you all to have a GREAT WEEKEND!

luv, nat

Posted by: Jenna
Re: school social TONIGHT!

Have a great time, Nat! I'm jealous . . . I'm stuck at my dad's again. Guess what we're having for dinner? That's right . . . takeout. xo Jenna

Posted by: Alyssa
Re: school social TONIGHT!

Aw, Jenna . . . well, at least it's takeout, and not, like, brussels sprouts, right? ;)

Have fun, Nat! You probably won't get this till later, so I hope you're having a great time . . . Alyssa

Hello everyone. I haven't written yet and I wanted to say hello. It's been busy here and it's strange to be in a new school after five years in elementary. I guess you guys all know how I'm feeling. (Except Brynn . . . lucky!) My favorite class this year is English, so far anyway. There's a lot of homework, but it's interesting. And I'm going to join the yearbook, I think.

Time for some good old-fashioned movie-and-popcorn night. Have a good weekend.

Your friend,

Karen

Natalie tapped her foot impatiently and crossed her arms. She was standing outside her apartment building, waiting for Hannah to arrive. Hannah, who was always on time, was already ten minutes late, and if she didn't show up soon, they were going to be late to the social! "Come on, Han . . ." Natalie muttered to herself. She looked uptown, then turned to look downtown, hoping to spot her friend's trademark cornrows, but Hannah was nowhere to be seen.

After she waited five minutes more, Natalie turned with a frustrated sigh to go back into her building and try calling Hannah's house. Just then, there was a tap on her shoulder. "Nat, I'm so sorry," Hannah said, out of breath. "There was all kinds of traffic, and the cab went the wrong way—"

"It's okay, Hannah," Natalie said. "But we'd better get going. The dance already started!"

"I wish you wouldn't call it that," Hannah grumbled as the girls walked down the street to the corner, where they'd catch a cab.

"That's what it is, though," Natalie said. "I mean, it's a social or whatever, true. But there will be dancing. Therefore, it is a dance."

"Yeah, but it makes it sound so *formal*," Hannah said. "Like people are bringing dates or something." She looked away, and then walked to the curb and raised her arm into the air. Almost immediately, a yellow cab pulled up next to the girls. Hannah opened the back door and slid across the leather seat. As Natalie got in next to her, Hannah told the cab driver the address of their school.

Moments later, they pulled up in front of the building. Excited, Natalie paid the driver and the girls hopped out and ran up to the front door, where their friends Erin and Kaitlyn were waiting. "Hey, guys!" Natalie said.

"Hey!" Kaitlyn said. "Natalie, Kyle's here . . . he's already inside!"

"Awesome," Natalie replied. "Let's go in! Is there any food? I'm starving . . ."

"There's pizza and stuff," Erin said, pulling the heavy door open and holding it so that the other three girls could pass by her and go in.

"I'm hungry too," Hannah said. "I had the worst cab ride on the way to Natalie's." She filled the girls in as they walked through the front hallway of the school and into the gymnasium. Once just inside the gym doors, they all paused: Half the gym was packed with kids dancing and eating, and half the room had been set up so that people could play basketball.

"Sweet, I want to shoot hoops!" Erin said.

Natalie laughed, looking at her friend, who was wearing boots with high heels and a cute red skirt. "In that outfit?" she asked teasingly.

"Sure, why not?" Erin replied nonchalantly. She swung her hair behind her shoulder. "Well . . . I have some sneakers in my locker," she added, smiling.

"I'm going to grab some pizza. Anybody want me to get them a slice?" Hannah asked.

"I'm going to go dance," Kaitlyn said. "Matt's already here." She smiled slyly. Matt, Nat knew, was the guy Kaitlyn had had a crush on since fourth grade.

"Have fun!" Natalie told her. "I'd love a slice of pizza, Han . . . I'll grab seats for us over there," she said, pointing toward the far end of the gym, where a few tables had been set up. Hannah nodded agreeably and headed toward the pizza, and Natalie started walking across the gym to the tables, looking for familiar faces as she crossed the squeaky wood floor. She smiled as she spotted Kyle, playing basketball with a couple of his friends. He noticed Natalie as she walked, and waved at her with a big grin on his face. They hadn't had much of a chance to talk yet at school, despite Natalie's best efforts. It was a much bigger school than she was used to, and the dance would be the first time she saw many of her friends.

Natalie waved back and headed over to say hello.

"Hey, Kyle!" she said, grinning. "How's the game going?"

"Pretty good," he said, scooping up the basketball and walking over to her. "I'm winning."

"You're totally not winning," one of his friends said teasingly.

"Whatever," Kyle replied. "Hey, Nat, can I come talk to you in a little while?"

Natalie's stomach filled with butterflies. "Of course!" she replied. "I'd better go find Hannah now."

"See you later," Kyle said, smiling.

Natalie scanned the room for her friend and finally saw Hannah sitting alone at a table across the gymnasium. As Nat walked across the room to Hannah, she took in all the noise—the music playing, sneakers squeaking, basketballs punching the floor, laughter, and talking. And Kyle was going to come by and talk to her! She couldn't get over how lucky she was feeling.

She sat down across from Hannah. "Where were you?" Hannah asked quietly.

"Just saying hi to Kyle," Natalie said.

"Oh. I thought you weren't coming over, or something." Hannah gestured to one of the plates sitting on the table, holding a big slice of pizza. "Anyway, they only had broccoli or mushroom, so I got you the mushroom. I couldn't remember if you liked them or not, but I figured you'd rather pick off mushrooms than broccoli. They're easier to pull out in one piece."

"I love mushrooms. Thanks, Hannah!" Natalie said, reaching for one of the plates. The pizza looked good—big slices of classic New York thin-crust pizza. It was covered with mushrooms, and just greasy enough that the paper plate below it was slightly orange. "Yum . . . this looks delicious!" she added. She raised the pizza to her mouth for a huge bite.

The music playing in the gym was loud and fast, a hip-hop song Natalie didn't know. "What is this song?" she asked Hannah.

"Oh, it was *huge* this summer," Hannah said excitedly. "It's Usher's latest single."

"What's it called?" Natalie asked.

"Um . . . I actually don't know," Hannah said, laughing. "I was in Europe, remember? If it ever played on the radio there, the DJ said the title in a different language."

Natalie laughed. "Well, I like it," she said.

"Me too," Hannah said cheerfully.

"Me too," a boy's voice added. Natalie swung around and saw Kyle standing there. "It's called 'Confessions.' It actually came out last year."

"Oh," Hannah said, her voice suddenly much colder.

What's up with that? Natalie thought. She decided to ignore the change in Hannah's tone, hoping that Kyle didn't notice it. "Hey, Kyle!" she exclaimed. "Are you having a good time?"

"For sure," Kyle said, shoving his hands in his pockets. He looked at Hannah and smiled. "I just beat Matt in a game of Horse. Plus I've had, like, twelve pieces of pizza."

"Cool," Hannah said sarcastically.

Kyle looked a little hurt, so Natalie hastily added, "How many letters did you win by?"

"Oh, two," Kyle said proudly. "S and E."

"Nice!" Nat said. She looked at Hannah, who seemed upset for some reason. "That's good, right, Hannah?" she prompted.

"Yeah, awesome," Hannah replied flatly.

The music changed from the Usher song to a slower, more romantic song. "Hey, um, Natalie . . . do you want to dance?" Kyle asked shyly.

Surprised, Natalie looked up at him. "Sure!" she said. She stood up, those butterflies floating through her stomach again, and they walked together to the dance floor, where Kyle tentatively put his arms around her waist, and she put her hands on his shoulders. They swayed back and forth to the rhythm of the song, and Nat could feel her heart pounding. She hadn't been this excited and nervous since the last time she saw Simon—back at camp! Would boys always have this effect on her?

As the song drew to a close, though, Natalie caught sight of Hannah, sitting all alone at the table, looking miserable. The song ended, and Natalie said, "I think I'm gonna go back and sit with Hannah. Would you mind grabbing me another slice of pizza? Vegetarian, if they have any."

"No prob," Kyle said. He smiled and took off toward the food, and Natalie walked back to where Hannah sat dejectedly.

"Hannah, are you okay?" Natalie asked softly.

"Yeah, I'm fine," Hannah replied.

"What's going on?"

"I don't know," Hannah admitted. She paused for a moment, looking around the crowded room. "I guess it's the boyfriend thing."

"What do you mean?" Natalie asked, surprised.

"Well . . ." Hannah paused. "I thought you were coming to the dance to hang out with me."

"I am hanging out with you!" Natalie exclaimed. She was quiet for a minute. "But . . . I mean, I only see Kyle for a few minutes during school, and I was excited to see him tonight, too."

"I guess it's true that when girls get boyfriends,

they stop wanting to see their best friends," Hannah said sadly.

The butterflies that had been swimming in Nat's stomach suddenly disappeared, turning into confusion. "Hannah, he's not my boyfriend," Natalie replied. "And anyway, I was only dancing with him for one song."

"Well, whatever. He will be. Him and Simon, too. And I'll be sitting alone at a table like a loser," Hannah replied angrily, looking down at her pizza.

Natalie didn't say anything for a moment. "Hannah, you're being silly," she said gently. Suddenly, a paper plate with a slice of mushroom pizza on it was placed onto the table in front of her, and she whipped around to see Kyle standing there, looking equally as hurt as Hannah.

"Who's Simon?" he asked in a low, angry voice, before spinning around and walking away, through the dancing couples and toward the basketball hoops.

Natalie's heart sank as she watched Kyle walk away. She only felt worse when she turned and saw the dejected look on Hannah's face. "Nat, I'm really sorry. I think I'm just going to go home," Hannah said sadly.

"But we've only been here for, like, twenty minutes!" Natalie said. *Not to mention, you totally just scared away the boy I like!* But she knew she couldn't say that out loud. Not with Hannah feeling so sensitive. *Talk about a lose-lose situation*, she thought, frustrated.

"Yeah, I know. I'm just really tired. I guess I'm not used to being back in school yet," Hannah replied. She stood up, not looking Natalie in the eye. "Bye," she said.

"Bye, Hannah," Natalie said sadly. She looked around the crowded gym. Erin was playing basketball— even in a skirt, she was making tons of baskets—and

Kaitlyn was dancing with Matt. Suddenly Natalie didn't feel like being at the dance either. She looked at her plate of pizza and even though she'd been starving when they arrived at the dance, she couldn't imagine eating another bite. She stood up, walked across the gym and through the front hallway of the school, pushed open the heavy front door, and stood outside, scanning the street for a cab.

As she walked toward the curb to hail a cab, she felt a hand on her shoulder.

"Wait up, Natalie," Kyle said. He looked down at his feet. "Tell me the truth. Do you have another boyfriend?"

Natalie felt very confused. Why was this so hard? "I don't have any boyfriend, Kyle," she said. Technically, at least, it *was* the truth.

"Okay," Kyle said, smiling tentatively. "I just wanted to make sure. Because . . . well . . ."

A cab stopped at the corner and Kyle escorted Natalie into it. Just like that, all thoughts of Simon—and Hannah—were gone. The butterflies were back. As the cab whizzed toward her building, Natalie realized that Kyle had never finished his sentence. But that was just fine. He didn't have to.

chapter FOUR

Jenna> SUNDAY

Jenna slammed shut the passenger door of her dad's car and started to trudge up the sidewalk to her mom's house. Adam and Stephanie lagged behind, carrying their bags and shouting good-byes to their father as he pulled out of the driveway.

Opening the front door and tossing her duffel bag down onto the floor, Jenna felt exhausted. It wasn't like her weekend had tired her out—just like last weekend, she'd watched a bunch of movies and eaten a lot of junk food. She'd done her homework, and spent tons of time online. Her dad had even let her order a cute new pair of shoes she'd found. But none of it had been tiring. She was just tired, already, after only two weeks of being shuttled back and forth between her mom and dad. And she was tired of her dad trying to make up for the divorce by being Superdad, and tired of getting used to a new house.

Jenna's mom walked out of the kitchen and gave her a hug. "Welcome back, sweetie!" she said. She hugged Adam and Stephanie, too. "Bring your stuff up to your rooms, kiddos," she went on. "Steph, I wrote down some phone messages for you, and Jenna, Nicole called last night. She said you didn't have to call her back."

"Do you know what she wanted?" Jenna asked, reaching down to take hold of the strap of her bag. She hefted it onto her shoulder.

"No, honey, she didn't say," her mom replied.

"Okay, thanks," Jenna said. She followed Adam and Stephanie up the stairs and went into her room.

She put her bag down on her bed and slowly started to unpack it, lifting out the folded shirts and jeans that were inside. Once she was unpacked, she slid the duffel under her bed and crossed the room to sit at her desk. She picked up the phone, but Stephanie was on the extension in her room. "Steph?" Jenna asked tentatively. "Are you going to be on long? I have to call Nicole."

"Just a couple of minutes," Stephanie said. "I'll knock on your door when I'm done. Or you can use Mom's line."

"It's okay, I'll wait," Jenna said, and set down the receiver. She turned on her computer, which always took a while to start up, so she paced around her room for a moment. There was a knock on her door, and Steph walked in, quietly closing the door behind her.

"I missed so many parties this weekend," Stephanie said, sighing as she flopped down onto Jenna's bed. She lowered her voice to almost a whisper. "Jen, I'm sick of going to Dad's."

"Me too," Jenna confided, sitting down next to her big sister and slumping down with her head in her hands. "I made plans with Nicole to hang out tonight, but we didn't get back in time . . . I was supposed to call her at seven, and it's almost nine thirty."

Stephanie made a sympathetic cluck. "That really stinks, Jenna," she said. She straightened up suddenly. "Hey, maybe if we ask Mom, we can stay home next weekend!"

Jenna sat up. "Really?" she asked. "Do you think she'd go for it?"

Stephanie shrugged. "Maybe," she said. "It's definitely worth a shot. We'll just explain that we haven't felt very settled in—we just got back from camp and we've had to be shuttled all over the place. I bet she won't care."

"Okay!" Jenna exclaimed hopefully. "Can we go ask her now?"

"Definitely," Steph agreed. She paused. "The only thing, though, is that I don't want to hurt Dad's feelings. So we can't try to get out of going to his place every weekend. Just this once."

"Just this once," Jenna repeated. She smiled. "Let's go talk to Mom."

They walked down the hallway to their mother's room and Steph rapped gently on the door. "Mom?" she called quietly. "Can we come in?"

"Sure, Steph," their mom's voice came through the door.

Stephanie pushed the door open. Their mother was lying in bed, reading a book. She slid a piece of paper into the book to mark her spot, and rested it on the bed next to her. Jenna and Stephanie sat down on the foot of the bed. "Mom, we . . ." Jenna looked at Steph for support. Her big sister nodded encouragingly. "We have something to ask," Jenna went on.

"What's up?" her mom asked.

"Well, Mom," Steph began, "we were wondering if we could stay home next weekend, instead of going to Dad's."

Their mother frowned. "Why?" she asked, sitting up. "Are you guys not having fun with your father?"

"No, it's not that," Jenna said slowly. "It's just that we just got back from camp, and we had to go straight to school, and I was supposed to—"

"We're just feeling like we haven't had time to adjust to being home," Stephanie said, interrupting Jenna. She threw Jenna a look. "It's just that."

Their mom looked concerned. "Well, I'm sorry, girls, but I can't make that decision. You know very well that it's been hard for your dad to move away from you, and it wouldn't be fair if I called him and told him you weren't coming for the weekend. He looks forward to his time with you. I know if the situation were reversed, there's no way I'd give up a minute with you kids. I'm sorry, but for now at least, you're spending weekends at your dad's. You'll readjust, I know you will. I know it's hard."

Jenna and Steph looked at each other. "But, Mom," Jenna began.

"Honey, I'm very sorry that this is the way things are," her mom said, cutting her off. "And your dad is too. But this is just how it has to be right now." She picked up her book and opened it to the page she'd marked, signaling the end of their conversation.

Jenna sighed. "Fine," she muttered. She slid off the foot of the bed and stomped out, not waiting to see how Stephanie would take the news.

When she arrived at school the next morning and

was shoving her things into her locker, Nicole walked up to her. "What happened to you last night?" Nicole asked.

Jenna rolled her eyes. "Dad made us go out to eat, so we were late getting home," she replied. "I was going to call you, but Steph was on the phone."

"Oh," Nicole said, twirling a strand of hair between her fingers. "I wish you hadn't been gone this weekend—I ended up having the most awesome party at my place on Saturday night. Everybody—everybody—was there! It was really fun."

"You had a party?" Jenna exclaimed, closing her locker and turning to face her friend. "Why didn't you tell me on Friday?"

"It was sort of a last-minute thing," Nicole said nonchalantly. She reached into her bag and pulled out a pack of gum. "Want some?" she asked, offering the pack to Jenna.

"Sure," Jenna said, reaching for a stick. "Thanks."

"So anyway," Nicole went on, taking out a stick of gum for herself and unwrapping it, "it was really cool. I had, like, fifteen people over and we watched movies and stuff. Like I said, I wish you could've been there. I called your house thinking maybe you'd decided to stay home from your dad's, but your mom said you were gone."

"Yeah," Jenna said sadly. "I was gone."

"Are you going to be around this weekend, you think?" Nicole asked. She hefted her backpack onto her shoulder. "Because I was thinking about having another party!"

Jenna sighed. "I don't know," she said. "My mom said I had to go to my dad's, but I really don't want to. It's boring there! So . . . I guess I'll let you know later this week."

"Cool," Nicole said with a laugh. "I really wish you could've come on Saturday, so I hope you're around this weekend! I've got to get to homeroom—see ya!"

"Bye," Jenna responded. She turned and walked toward her class, thinking, *It isn't fair at all. My parents are the ones who split up—why am I the one who's suffering?*

At lunch, Jenna slid onto a bench next to Nicole. She unwrapped her sandwich slowly, and took a bite of the bologna on wheat toast with mustard—her favorite.

"Everybody's talking about your party," she said.

"Yeah, I know," Nicole said. She bit her lip. "Jen, I really wish you could've been there. Why don't you ask if you can stay home this weekend?"

Jenna sighed and looked down at her sandwich. "Nicole, I really want to. I asked my mom last night if I could stay home next weekend and she said no. She said I just have to get used to this, basically."

Nicole sighed. "Well, maybe she'll change her mind," she said consolingly. "Over here!" she called suddenly. Jenna looked up to see her friend motioning to a group of girls who had just walked into the cafeteria. Molly, Veronica, and Lisa strolled over and set their lunch bags down on the table. "What's up, guys?" Nicole said excitedly.

"Oh my God, Nic . . ." Molly said. "You know how I was talking to Brad at the party?"

"Yeah?" Nicole prompted, her voice lowered.

"Well, he came up to me at my locker today!" Molly exclaimed.

"Awesome!" Nicole replied. "What did he say?"

"He asked if I was going to go to your house again next weekend," Molly said. "Do you think you'll have another party?"

"Um, why not?" Nicole said. "Saturday night."

"Awesome!" Veronica shrieked. "Are you going to come this time, Jenna?"

Jenna looked down at her half-eaten sandwich. "I have to go to my dad's," she said. "I don't think I can go."

"That stinks!" Lisa said. "Nicole's parties are super fun."

"That's what I hear," Jenna mumbled.

"Can't you, like, fake sick or something?" Nicole said. Her face lit up. "You know, you could pretend like you were sick on Friday, and then you wouldn't have to go to your dad's, and then if you told you, mom you were feeling better on Saturday, you could come!"

Jenna thought about it. That just might work! "Maybe . . ." she said tentatively. "I mean, it seems like that might work. . . ." She had *promised* her parents no more pranks. But this wouldn't be quite a prank . . . would it?

"You definitely should do it," Lisa agreed.

The bell rang then, and the girls got up. "You should start faking sick a little bit now," Nicole suggested as they walked toward their lockers. "That way nobody will suspect when Friday rolls around . . . and you just don't feel so good. . . ." She pantomimed rubbing her belly in pain and rolled her eyes, pressing her hand to her forehead.

Jenna laughed. "I don't know," she said. "Seems pretty risky . . . but it might be worth it."

Alex> MONDAY

The bell for fifth period rang and Alex hurried to get to her class, pushing past people in her effort to make it to English on time. When she was nearing the classroom, her friend Lucy came running up to her. She grabbed Alex's arm. "Alex, I just heard that they posted the soccer teams!" she said, out of breath. "Let's go look!"

Alex was unsure. "But class is about to start—" she began.

"The soccer coach is there—she'll write you a pass," Lucy said. "Come on!"

"Okay," Alex agreed. She took Lucy's hand and they ran down the hall toward the girls' locker room.

There was a crowd of girls inside, standing around the big bulletin board next to the coach's office. Alex pushed her way to the front of the crowd and scanned the board for her name.

There were three pieces of paper on the bulletin board, each listing a different group of girls: those who had made the team, those who hadn't, and those who would have to go back that afternoon for one more round of tryouts. Alex first looked down the list of people who hadn't made the team, and was totally relieved to not see her name there. Then she checked the list of people who had definitely made the team—but her name wasn't there, either. Alex's heart sunk deep into her stomach.

Coach Gregorson, a tall, redheaded woman who also taught Alex's PE class, was standing next to the bulletin board with a clipboard, assigning groups of girls who were on the third list to tryout teams. "Alex," Coach Gregorson called. "Come on over."

Alex walked over, feeling nervous. "Hi," she said.

"Hi, hon," Coach Gregorson said, looking down at her clipboard. "So, I'm going to put you on the A team for tryouts tonight. That will start at four. Is that okay?"

"Yes," Alex said. "Can I ask you a question?" Her stomach felt like it was in knots.

"Sure," the coach said, scribbling something onto her clipboard. "What's up?"

"Well," Alex began. "Um . . . it's just that in fifth grade, I was the MVP of my team . . ."

Coach smiled. "Don't worry, Alex," she said consolingly. "A lot of the girls who weren't immediately placed onto the team are nervous. You'll be fine, and if you don't make it, you'll try out again next year. No matter what, the second round gives me a better idea of what you can do, and it will give you valuable experience." She patted Alex on the shoulder. "See you at four." She grabbed her packet of passes out of her pocket and quickly scribbled one for Alex. Alex walked away, shoving her pass into her pocket.

Alex spent the last two periods of the day in a nervous haze. After school, she was so worried about the tryouts, she could hardly stand it. After the final bell rang, she put her books into her locker and walked around the halls aimlessly for a few minutes. Then she popped into the computer lab, since she knew she had an hour to kill, and checked into the Camp Lakeview blog.

Posted by: Val
Subject: Hi, everybody!

Sorry it's taken me so long to write anything other than a response! We didn't have Internet access for a while. Anyway, It's been cool to see what everyone is doing.

I'm back at school, having a great time—middle school is different, but it's so much fun! I've already met a bunch of new people—it's really great.

Love, Val

Alex wanted to post about the upcoming tryouts, about how nervous she was that she wouldn't make the team, about feeling like she wasn't good enough, and about how hard middle school was for her. But she just couldn't do it. She trusted and loved her camp friends so much, but she didn't want them to see her feeling like she might fail. She closed the browser window and got up.

After leaving the computer lab, she headed for the locker room, where she changed into her practice clothes. She pulled her hair back into a ponytail, tied her sneakers in double knots, and checked the time. It was three forty-five, fifteen minutes before her tryout was scheduled to begin. *I guess I'll go and watch the other group*, she thought, trying to get excited about playing.

Outside on the field, Coach Gregorson blew on her whistle. "That's enough, kids—great work today," she said, putting her hands on her hips. The group of girls gathered around her. "Okay. Coach Henry, Coach Lisa, and I will be talking to you about whether you've made the team, and if you have, what position you'll be playing and what your goals should be for the season. Please take a seat on the grass and come over when we call you. Let's start with Jane."

A girl with long, braided brown hair walked tentatively toward Coach Gregorson and Henry and Lisa, who were two high-school kids who helped Coach Gregorson. The other players scattered into small groups along the sidelines of the field. From her seat in the bleachers, Alex watched as the coaches sat down with Jane and talked to her. After a minute or so, Jane got up, looking really happy, and walked toward the school. Another girl walked over and sat down with the coaches, but it didn't go so well. After they talked to her for just a moment, the girl's face crumpled and she looked like she was going to cry. Seeing Jane make the team had made Alex feel a little better, but seeing this girl not make it brought the butterflies back to Alex's stomach.

A few more girls came and sat down on the bleachers with Alex. She knew one of them from her fifth-grade soccer team and they smiled nervously at each other. "Hey, Amanda," Alex said.

"Hi," Amanda replied. She sat down next to Alex. "I like your shoelaces."

Alex looked down at her shoes. She'd bought new yellow laces with smiley faces on them. "Thanks," she said. "They make me smile."

Amanda laughed. "That's good," she said. "Are you nervous?"

"Totally," Alex said. "Are you?"

"Yeah," Amanda admitted. "It's weird to have to try out, since we didn't have to in fifth grade."

"I know," Alex groaned. "I wish I would've just made it in the first cut!"

From the field, Coach Gregorson blew on her whistle. "All right, girls, let's get started!" she called, motioning for everyone to join her on the field.

When all the girls were assembled, the coach said, "Okay, we're going to start by warming up, and then we're going to play a short game so that we can see everyone's skills. You'll play the position you're used to. I split up the tryouts so that everyone would play the position they've played before. Does anyone have any questions?"

Alex looked around. One girl with short red curls raised her hand. "Yes, Debbie?" the coach asked.

"When will we find out whether we made the team?" Debbie asked tentatively.

The coach laughed. "Right after tryouts, we'll sit you down and talk with you. Don't worry about that right now, though—just have a good time." She blew on her whistle. "Let's warm up, everybody!"

Henry and Lisa walked to the center of the field, and all the girls followed. The two older kids led everyone through some simple exercises, like jumping jacks and sit-ups. Then they did some practice with the ball, passing it and pivoting and dribbling. Alex was starting to feel like she was getting a real workout, which was great—she loved the feeling of her heart pounding and sweat starting to build along her hairline.

After about ten minutes of warming up, Coach Gregorson blew her whistle. "Great work, girls," she called. "Let's split into teams now for the scrimmage. On team A, I have Alex, Amanda, Debbie, Carla, LaShondra, Franny, Cate, Michaela, Sara, Savannah, and Monica. Everyone else, you're on team B."

The group of girls split up, and the coaches walked to the sidelines. As the game began, Alex stopped feeling nervous. She ran fast and worked hard, and every time her team scored a point, she felt a little lighter. After playing for about twenty minutes, Coach Gregorson blew her whistle. "All right, that's great, everyone," she said. "We've made our decisions. We'll start with Amanda. Everyone else, relax on the field, do some stretches."

Alex sat down on the grass and stretched out her legs. Franny, who'd been on her team, sat down next to her. "That was fun, huh?" Franny said casually.

"Yeah," Alex said. "It was cool."

"Did you play at your old school?" Franny gently pulled a few blades of grass from the field.

"Yup," Alex replied. She looked over at Amanda, who looked sort of sad as the coach talked to her. Coach Gregorson patted Amanda on the shoulder, and then they both stood up. Amanda walked slowly toward the school building.

"All right, Alex?" Coach Gregorson called. "Come on over."

Suddenly, the butterflies returned to Alex's tummy. She slowly stood up and walked over to Coach Gregorson, Henry, and Lisa.

"Sit down, Alex," the coach said kindly. Alex sat down and crossed her legs, and Coach Gregorson followed suit.

"Henry, why don't you start?" Coach Gregorson asked.

"Okay. Alex, you obviously have played soccer before," Henry said, looking at his clipboard. "You've got good skills with the ball, and you're fast. That's really great."

"That is really great," Lisa put in. "We are a little worried that you aren't as skilled as some of the other players when it comes to strategy."

"I can learn that stuff!" Alex exclaimed. "I am a really fast—"

Coach Gregorson cut her off. "We know you can, Alex. You're on the team."

Relief flooded into Alex's body. "I am?" she asked tentatively.

"You are," Coach assured her. "But, to begin with, you might not get to play as much as some of the older girls. That isn't a bad thing. It just means that you need to pay attention and learn about game strategy. That's your goal for the year: Learn about strategy."

"I don't get to play?" Alex said softly.

"To begin with, you'll just watch. Then, when we feel like your performance in practice shows that you're learning, you'll play a little. It'll be hard work, Alex, but I know you can do it," Coach said, reaching over and patting her on the shoulder. "After all, all of our star players have to start somewhere. Any questions?"

Alex felt tears welling up. "No," she said quickly. "See you at practice tomorrow." She got up and walked to the school as fast as she could. She didn't bother to change out of her practice clothes; she just threw on her regular sneakers and put her school clothes into her bag. She couldn't believe how disappointed she was! She'd made the team, after all. But she wanted to play.

▲ ▲ ▲

Alex walked home quickly, and called to her mom, who was in the kitchen making dinner. "I made the team," she yelled.

Her mom came out of the kitchen, drying her hands on a dish towel. "Honey, that's great!" she said. "I'm so proud of you." She reached toward Alex for a hug, but Alex drew away.

"They said I wouldn't get to play, Mom," she said sadly.

"What?" her mom said, pulling away.

"They said I have to learn about strategy, and so my goal for the season is to learn about strategy, and if I do, I'll get to play a little."

"Oh, honey," her mom said, walking to Alex and wrapping her arms around her. "Don't worry, you'll show them how good you are, and you'll play before you know it."

"I know, Mom," Alex said. And she did know. That didn't stop her from feeling disappointed, though. She was used to being a star—it was going to be hard to start at the bottom.

"Dinner's almost ready, so why don't you go upstairs and change and wash up?"

"I'm not really hungry right now, actually. Is it okay if I eat later?"

With a concerned look on her face, Alex's mom nodded. "Sure, honey. I'll save a plate for you. Is your blood sugar okay?"

Alex sighed. She had to eat regular meals because of her diabetes, even when she wasn't hungry sometimes. "I feel fine. But I can check it. And I'll eat in a couple of hours or something."

"Okay, sweetheart. Come find me if you want to talk."

Alex picked up her bag and ran up the stairs to her room. She flopped down on the bed. Too exhausted to think about anything, she just fell asleep.

chapter
FIVE
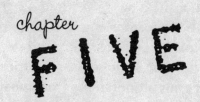

Grace> MONDAY

"Pass the pepper, please, honey," Grace's mom said. Grace's father handed the wooden pepper mill to Grace, who placed it into her mom's hand. Dinner was chicken, peas, and rice: Grace's favorite combo.

"How was school today, Grace?" her father asked between bites of his chicken.

"Um, well, I learned about ecosystems in science," Grace replied. "About how all life relies on other life and stuff, and food chains."

"That's interesting!" Grace's mother said.

"How is your English class going?" Grace's dad asked abruptly.

Grace took a big forkful of peas and chewed and swallowed before answering. "It's . . . it's okay," she replied slowly. "I've been working really hard, and I've been thinking about asking my camp friends if they want to do the book club again."

"What are you reading?" her dad asked.

"We're still reading *Hatchet*," Grace said. They

were almost done—she only had one more chapter to read. "And then next we're reading *The Pinballs*," Grace said. "That's the one I'm going to ask my friends at camp to read with me." She took another bite of rice. "I just want to read it at the same time as my friends."

"Aren't your school friends reading it, too?" her dad asked. "I think the book club is a good idea, but don't you also have friends at school who'll be reading it in the same class?"

Grace thought about her drama club friends, and how they were reading more advanced stuff. "No," she said. "Most of my friends are reading *Animal Farm*. They're in different classes."

"Then I think your book club idea is great," Grace's mom said. She shot a look at Grace's father, who was opening his mouth to say something. "Don't you, honey?"

"Yes," Grace's dad said. He looked at Grace's mom. "At any rate, your mother and I wanted to talk to you about something," he went on.

Grace's mom put down her fork and nodded. "We met with some people at your school today," she said gently. "Principal Snyder, the guidance counselor, and Mrs. Burr."

"You talked to my teacher about me?" Grace said, mortified. Did any of the teachers mention drama club?

"It was a good meeting, Grace," her father said, and Grace let out a sigh of relief. "They all said you're a hard worker, and that's great."

"Can they move me to a better class?" Grace asked.

"No, honey, they can't. They think, and your dad and I agree, that you need a little more work on your reading

68

before you can get bumped up a level. But that's okay! You're in a brand-new school, and you're already working hard." Grace's mom looked proud of her.

"They told us that you've been working hard, and speaking up more in class, which is great," Grace's dad continued. "We've also noticed that you've been making an effort. We're very proud of you for staying late at the library."

"Uh . . . right," Grace said. She felt a stab of guilt go through her. "The library." She'd forgotten that she told her parents that's where she was when she was really at drama club meetings. She'd even gone so far as to check out a stack of books that she left on her bedroom floor.

"Working hard like that really proves that you're growing up, and that you're really trying," Grace's dad went on. "And we've decided that if you can hold onto a B average until the end of the semester, we'll consider letting you join the drama club."

Grace looked up from her plate. "You will?" she said disbelievingly. "But you said that I wouldn't be able to until next year!"

Grace's parents exchanged a look. "I know. But we've talked about it quite a bit, and we were encouraged by your teachers today. They think you deserve a big reward if you can hold on to a B that long, and we agree."

Guilt crept up into Grace's tummy, and she put down her fork. "Well, that's really great, you guys, thanks," she said. "I'm full. Can I be excused?"

Grace's mom gave her a worried look. "Are you feeling okay?" she said. "Come here, let me feel your forehead."

"I'm fine, Mom, I'm just full," Grace said, pushing herself away from the table. She stood up, carried her plate to the trash, and dumped the leftover chicken and rice into the garbage. After sliding her plate into the dishwasher, she said, "Good dinner, Mom," and went upstairs to her room.

▲ ▲ ▲

Lying on her bed, Grace read a few pages of *Hatchet*, but then sighed and placed the book down on her pillow. She got up slowly and crossed the room to her desk, turning on the computer as she sat down at her desk chair.

She logged on to Instant Messenger, and instantly received a message from Natalie.

<NatalieNYC>: hey, grace!

<Grrrrace>: Hey, Nat

<NatalieNYC>: what's up?

<Grrrrace>: Not much, u?

<NatalieNYC>: oh, boy problems. how's school & drama club??

<Grrrrace>: It's really fun . . . I have a bunch of new friends and Em and I still talk all the time

<NatalieNYC>: i knew you would make friends no prob

<Grrrrace>: The bad thing is, I still have to lie to my parents

<NatalieNYC>: oh no, grace!

<Grrrrace>: Yeah. They said if I have a B average in English I can join second semester . . .

<NatalieNYC>: you can do it!

<Grrrrace>: Have you read *The Pinballs*?

<NatalieNYC>: yes!!! that's one of my favorites

<Grrrrace>: Would you want to read it again?

<NatalieNYC>: definitely! are you reading it?

<Grrrrace>: We start reading it next week

<NatalieNYC>: cool!

<Grrrrace>: Do you think maybe you'd read it with me, at the same time?

<NatalieNYC>: totally

<Grrrrace>: Really?

<NatalieNYC>: definitely. let's have a book club! i'll post about it on the lakeview blog tonight! you start it on monday?

<Grrrrace>: Yes.

<NatalieNYC>: awesome. so we'll start reading it monday!

<Grrrrace>: Thanks, Nat

<NatalieNYC>: no prob, grace. now, can you help me?

<Grrrrace>: With what?

<NatalieNYC>: my boy probs . . . .

<Grrrrace>: Definitely . . . what's going on?

<NatalieNYC>: oh man. where do I start?

Natalie and Grace chatted for an hour, and afterward, Grace crawled into her bed. She picked up *Hatchet* and started reading. The ending was the best part! Before Grace knew it, she was closing the book with a satisfying smack. She looked at the digital clock next to her bed. It was almost 10 PM, so Grace changed into her pajamas. Before getting into bed, she checked the Lakeview blog.

Posted by: Natalie
Subject: book club!

hey, everybody. grace and i were talking tonight and we thought it would be fun to start our book club again! our first book will be the pinballs and we'll start next monday. every night, post a little bit about what you think about the book! let us know if you want to join.

love,
nat

Posted by: Karen
Re: book club!

I am in.
Your friend, Karen

Posted by: Alyssa
Re: book club!

Me too!
xx A

Posted by: Sarah
Re: book club!

I LOVE that book. I'm in! Sarah

Posted by: Marissa
Re: book club!

Great idea, Nat and Grace! I loved that book. I'll totally read it again.
Love, Mars

It seemed as though everyone was signed up, except

Chelsea, but Grace just assumed she wasn't interested. That would be typical for the sometimes-snobby blonde. For the first time, Grace was excited to go to English class the next day. Not only had she finished *Hatchet*, but she was really excited to read *The Pinballs* . . . with a little help from her friends.

Jenna> TUESDAY

At the breakfast table Tuesday morning, while she ate cereal with her mom and Adam, Jenna decided to put her plan into action. She looked at her mom and Adam, and then coughed loudly.

Her mom lowered the morning paper and shot her a worried glance. "That doesn't sound good, honey," she said. "Are you coming down with something?"

Jenna took a spoonful of cereal and chewed slowly before answering. "I don't know," she said thoughtfully. "I mean, a couple of my friends have been sick . . ."

"Who?" Adam butted in. "I don't remember anyone being sick."

"Just people at school," Jenna replied through gritted teeth, throwing him a look. "Like . . . Helen."

"Who's Helen?" Adam asked, clearly dubious.

"She's in my math class, Adam," Jenna said, her teeth getting even tighter. "She sits next to me in my *math* class." She knew that would bother her brother, who hadn't passed the test to take the advanced class, Algebra 1, and was stuck in the regular sixth-grade math class.

She was right. Adam dropped his gaze and picked

up his glass of juice. "Oh," he said. "I don't know her."

Jenna's mom looked over her newspaper. "What's wrong with Helen?" she asked, folding the paper and setting it down on the empty chair next to her.

"I don't know, she was out yesterday," Jenna lied, feeling a guilty blush creep across her face. Helen didn't really exist at all—it was just the first name that came to her mind. "And so was Tanya, who you also don't know, Adam," she added, deepening the lie. "On Friday," she continued, "they were at school but they were coughing a lot."

"Did they go to Nicole's party?" Adam asked in his best innocent voice. He put down his spoon and stared right at Jenna.

She narrowed her eyes. "I don't know, Adam. I wasn't there," she said pointedly. Before anyone could ask her any more questions, she noisily took a big bite of cereal and chomped on it loudly for way longer than she needed to. As soon as she swallowed, she immediately shoved another spoonful into her mouth.

But her mom didn't get the hint. "I didn't know Nicole had a party, Jen!" she said. "When was it?"

Jenna's mouth was full, so she couldn't respond, but Adam's spoon still rested on the table. He crossed his arms. "It was last Saturday," he said. "Everybody at school was talking about it, about how fun it was and stuff."

"That's too bad you had to miss it, sweetheart," Jenna's mom said consolingly.

Jenna swallowed. "Yeah, whatever, it's fine," she said. "Adam, let's get going, we're going to be late." She shoved her bowl away from her, and stood up quickly.

"Do you need a ride?" her mom asked. "Steph and Matt left already, but I can drive you if you need me to."

"That's okay, Mom," Jenna said. She started walking toward the door, but stopped and thought for a moment. "Actually . . . maybe I do want to get a ride. I don't know if being out in the cold will be good for me." She coughed again, more gently this time.

She looked over at Adam, who was slowly shaking his head at her. He could always tell when she had something up her sleeve. Narrowing her eyes, Jenna added, "I hope Helen is back in math today . . . we were going to work together on a project."

Their mom stood up from the table and began clearing away the breakfast dishes. Jenna walked through the living room and into the entrance hall, where her shoes and backpack were. She knelt down to slip on her sneakers and tied the laces into double knots. As she was straightening up and sliding her backpack onto her shoulders, Adam walked into the hallway.

"Are you faking?" he accused her.

"I'm not!" Jenna replied defensively. She pushed her hair out of her eyes. "I am feeling sick."

"That was the worst cough I've ever heard in my life," Adam said. He bent down to put on his sneakers. "If this is just another prank—if you're trying to get out of going to Dad's so you can go to Nicole's party—well, I don't think it's gonna fly. Mom wasn't born yesterday."

"I'm not!" Jenna exclaimed angrily. "I am feeling sick!"

The jingle of their mom's car keys floated in from the living room. Jenna lowered her voice. "Anyway, just stay out of it, Adam," she said. "I don't feel well and you're making me feel worse."

Adam stood up and put on his backpack. "You'll feel even worse if you have to stay home all weekend and Mom doesn't let you go out on Saturday because you're sick," he pointed out. "Just wait."

"Wait for what?" their mom said, entering the room. She shrugged her black trench coat on. "Ready?"

"Nothing, Mom," Jenna said. "Yeah. I'm ready."

"Me too," Adam said. "Let's go."

Their mom walked out the front door, and Adam and Jenna followed. Jenna let the door slam softly as she closed it. She walked down the driveway and got into the backseat of her mom's SUV.

▲ ▲ ▲

Jenna didn't talk to her brother on the ride to school, and when their mom pulled up in front of the school building, she jumped out of the car, yelling a quick good-bye and adding a small cough for good measure. Without waiting for Adam, she ran into the building.

She had a few minutes before she had to be in homeroom, so Jenna walked to the library. The night before, she'd gotten excited about Natalie's posting on the blog. She was so happy to be part of the book club. She browsed through the library's stacks, and finally found *The Pinballs* and checked it out at the desk. "Great book!" the librarian, a tall, slender woman with curly black hair, said.

"I'm reading it with some friends," Jenna told her.

"That's great!" the librarian responded. "I'm in a book club, too."

"Really?" Jenna asked. "Is it fun?"

"Definitely," the librarian said happily. "We get together, eat snacks, and talk about books—it's great!" She laughed, and Jenna laughed with her.

"Well, my book club is over the Internet," Jenna admitted. "But I'm excited for it to start. I'd better go. I'll be late to class!"

"Enjoy the book," the librarian told her.

Jenna stopped by her locker to drop off her bag. She planned on bringing the book to homeroom, so she could get a head start. On her way to the classroom, Nicole ran up to her.

"Hey, Jen!" Nicole said, falling into step beside Jenna.

"Hi!" Jenna replied.

"Did you talk to your mom about this weekend?" Nicole asked, stepping out of the way of some boys walking in a pack down the hall.

"No . . ." Jenna said impishly. "But . . . I did start coughing a lot!" She laughed as Nicole's eyes lit up.

"You did? Do you think she bought it?"

"Yeah, totally. I told her some of my friends at school were sick." They stopped outside Jenna's homeroom. "See you at lunch?"

"Definitely! See you later!" Nicole said. "Bye!"

A strange feeling of guilt crept into Jenna's stomach. She knew that a few faked coughs weren't exactly lies, but they weren't telling the truth, either. Was it worth it, just to go to a party? She hated to lie, but she also hated the idea that everyone would be hanging out without her. Maybe Adam was on to something—not with drop-ping it, of course, but with thinking of it as just another prank. Pranks were harmless, right? Except for that one at Lakeview that didn't go exactly as planned. . . .

She pushed the bad feeling out of her mind and walked into homeroom just in time for roll call.

chapter SIX

natalie> TUESDAY

After school, Natalie found Hannah at her locker. They hadn't talked to each other the day before, and Nat really hoped Hannah wasn't still upset about the school dance. "Hey, Han," she said tentatively.

Hannah smiled and closed her locker. "Hi, Natalie." She took a deep breath. "I'm sorry about Friday. I didn't mean to get you in trouble with Kyle. I was just having a bad day."

"It's okay," Natalie said. "I talked to Kyle after you left. So everything is fine with me and him. I just hope everything is okay with me and you!"

"It is," Hannah said. "Want to walk home together?"

"Of course," Natalie said, feeling hugely relieved. "Let's go!"

▲ ▲ ▲

"I mean, ever since that day when we bumped into each other in the mess hall at camp, Simon and

I hung out all the time," Natalie said as she and Hannah slowly walked up Fifth Avenue. "So I don't understand why he hasn't called, or e-mailed, or anything!"

"Yeah, that's weird," Hannah said, slowing to peek into a store window displaying lots of colorful bags and shoes.

"I would call him, of course," Natalie went on, "but I don't want to be too pushy. And I did send him an e-mail right after we got back from camp, but I haven't heard anything."

The girls came to a crosswalk and waited for the light to change. "I don't think you should worry, Nat," Hannah said.

As the "don't walk" signal changed, they stepped into the street. "Yeah. And now that I think about it, Jenna did tell me that her brother talked to Simon—they were in the same bunk—after we got back from camp, and he said that he misses me. Which just makes this more confusing, really, right? If he misses me, why doesn't he call? And if he doesn't miss me, why did he say that he did?"

"Why don't you just call him?" Hannah asked. "Oooh, let's get ice cream!" She stopped outside the ice cream store's window. "They have coconut today! Our favorite!"

"Okay!" Natalie exclaimed.

They went into the shop and ordered two small cones of coconut—with chocolate sprinkles, of course—from the man standing behind the counter. While they waited for him to scoop their ice cream, Hannah said, "I didn't even ask you how the rest of the dance went on Friday."

Natalie looked at her. "Uh . . . I left right after you did, Hannah," she said slowly.

"You did? Why?"

"After we had that talk, I didn't feel like staying," Natalie admitted. She looked down at the floor.

"Okay, girls, two coconut cones, chocolate sprinkles. That'll be four dollars," the old man behind the counter said. He smiled at them.

Natalie pulled a five-dollar bill out of her purse. "You can pay me back later," she said to Hannah. She handed over the bill and got a dollar in return, which she shoved into the man's tip jar.

"Good-bye, ladies!" he said.

They left, and the bell over the door jingled as the door swung shut.

In the street, they paused to take bites of their ice cream before continuing to walk uptown along the avenue. "So . . . why'd you leave, Nat?" Hannah said tentatively. "The dance, I mean."

"Because my best friend left!" Natalie exclaimed.

"Right," Hannah replied sheepishly. She licked her ice cream. "I guess it was pretty silly of me to get so upset that you were going to ditch me for a boy."

"It was," Natalie said, mock-sternly. "And anyway, it was two boys."

▲ ▲ ▲

Natalie was home that evening relaxing when her cell phone rang. She didn't recognize the number on the caller ID.

"Hello?" Natalie said.

"Hi, Nat," a boy's voice said on the other end.

"Hi . . . who's this?"

"It's Kyle," he said. "I'm calling from my mom's

phone since mine is out of batteries."

"Hey, Kyle, what's up?" Natalie said, feeling nervous and excited. A phone call from a boy! This was huge!

"Uh," Kyle paused. "I was calling to ask if you want to go Rollerblading in the park tomorrow, but if you have plans or you don't want to, it's okay, and maybe I'll just see you at school then," he continued, not taking a breath as he rattled off his words.

Natalie laughed. "I'd love to go Rollerblading tomorrow!"

"You would?" Kyle said, surprised.

"Definitely!" Nat replied. "I love Rollerblading."

"You do?" Kyle stammered. "Um . . . cool! So, I was thinking we could just go after school, and maybe we could get ice cream or something, and then since I live near you I would walk you home."

"Sounds great, Kyle . . . I'll see you at school tomorrow!" Natalie was excited already.

"Cool. Bye, Nat," Kyle said.

"Bye!"

I can't believe it! A date with Kyle! she thought excitedly. *Better call Hannah to plan my outfit!* But as she picked up her cell phone to punch in Hannah's number, she started to have second thoughts. She and Hannah had just made up that afternoon—the whole dating thing might still be a sore topic. The idea of having to keep her first date—her first date!—to herself was totally depressing, but she knew it was the right thing to do for now.

I'm still waiting from the phone call from Simon, Natalie realized. Was it really worth it?

To: MarissaRox
From: NatalieNYC
Subject: help . . .

hey, marissa—
i am desperate for some advice from someone older
and wiser (and cooler!), like yourself. my best friend, hannah,
has been acting really weird since i got home. she keeps
making snide comments about me liking two boys at once
(simon, obviously, and kyle, from school).
on friday at the dance, kyle overheard hannah talking
about simon. i smoothed it over, though, and told him i didn't
have any boyfriends at all. and today, kyle called and asked
me to go rollerblading with him in central park tomorrow, and
hannah got really mad at me and said that i was acting like
she wasn't important. then she stormed out. i don't know
what to do. can you help?
luv, nat

From: MarissaRox
To: NatalieNYC
Subject: Re: help . . .

Hey, Nat! It's good to hear from you. Sounds like
lots of exciting stuff is happening in your life! How fun to go
Rollerblading in Central Park. . . . I'm jealous! I'm up to my ears
in homework over here . . .
Here's what I think is going on with Hannah: She's
afraid you're growing up faster than she is. If I were in your
shoes——I'd have really cute shoes! Just kidding . . . And also,
I'd make sure Hannah knows that you aren't outgrowing her. It
sounds like that's what she's worried about. Take time to do

things with her that don't involve boys at all. (And I know you already know this, but don't rush into the boy thing yourself! You've got so much time!)

Let me know if I can help any more, hon. Love to hear from you.

Love, Marissa

▲ ▲ ▲

Alex> TUESDAY

Alex was in a great mood as she entered the locker room and began changing into her clothes for soccer practice. She'd had a pretty good day at school, and it was really warm and sunny outside. She couldn't wait for the first day of practice to get underway!

As she slipped her jersey over her head and leaned down to tie her shoes, Alex thought about practice, wondering how it would go. She straightened up and pulled her hair into two pigtails, securing them with two purple elastics that she'd had on her wrist. Then she shoved her school clothes into her locker, slammed it shut, and locked it.

As she walked through the locker room to the door that led to the practice field, she passed a group of four older girls. One of them, a girl named Cindy who had short blond hair, snickered as Alex walked by. "Nice hair," she said.

Alex whipped around, wanting to fire back a retort, but the confident, mean looks on the faces of Cindy and her friends stopped her. The older girls laughed again as Alex slunk out the door red-faced.

Outside, she immediately pulled the elastics out of her hair and pulled it into a long, sleek ponytail. "That was so mean," she said under her breath. She smoothed down her practice jersey and shook her head to clear it, then walked toward the field.

When she had passed the bleachers, she heard the older girls behind her, snickering and laughing. "Oh look," Cindy said, "she has grown-up hair now!" Alex wished she was the kind of girl who would respond, but she wasn't. She just steeled her shoulders and continued to walk onto the field.

There were about ten girls waiting for practice to begin. Alex recognized most of them from tryouts, and walked over to a girl named Trish, who was in her English class. Trish was a tall girl with light brown hair that fell to her shoulders. She'd used barrettes to pull her bangs out of her eyes for practice. "Hey, Trish," Alex said shyly.

"Hi, Alex," Trish said. "Could you believe the homework in English today?"

"I know," Alex replied. "I don't know how I'm going to get it all done!" Their teacher had assigned the class an essay on someone important in their lives, and it had to be three pages long. To make matters worse, it was due on Thursday, giving Alex only two days to write it. "Who are you going to write about?" she asked Trish.

Trish shrugged. "Maybe my mom? I don't really know," she said. "What about you?"

"I have no idea," Alex said. She sighed. "I can't believe it's only the second week of school and I already have so much homework to do."

"Yeah," Trish responded. "I guess that's middle school for you." They shared a commiserating look.

Just then, Coach Gregorson walked onto the field, followed by Henry and Lisa. Alex could already tell that she was going to look up to Lisa a lot. The older girl seemed so calm and confident. As she walked onto the field, her ponytail swung from side to side, and she was smiling.

Coach blew on her whistle. "All right, team," she said. "We're going to start warming up now. Please stretch out, and then we'll get moving."

Alex and Trish sat down on the field and stretched out their legs. As Alex reached for her toes, Trish whispered, "Are you going to get to start, do you think? In the games?"

Alex whispered back, "No. I don't think so." She looked over at Trish. "What about you?"

"They said I could if I learn some stuff," Trish confided.

"Me too," Alex said. She switched legs, stretching her left leg out and reaching toward it with her arms.

"Okay," Coach Gregorson said. "Let's start with some running. Henry, please go stand midfield," she said, pointing. "Everyone, when I blow my whistle, run to Henry, and then run back, five times."

Alex stood up next to Trish and shook out her arms, jogging in place for a moment. When the coach's whistle blew, she took off toward Henry, running fast enough to keep up with the group but not so fast that she'd lose too much energy. As she ran, sweat began to form on her forehead. She pulled ahead of Trish after the first lap, and heard Henry call, "Nice pace, Alex!"

After the five laps, Lisa had brought out a big bag of balls that she handed out to the group. "Okay," she said. "Everybody, please pair up, and let's practice some passes."

Alex looked at Trish, who nodded at her happily. Lisa threw Trish a ball, and she and Alex walked a few paces away to begin kicking the ball back and forth to each other.

As Alex ran around, returning the ball to Trish every time, her worries about not being able to play in the games started to dissipate. She didn't notice Cindy and one of her friends watching her, and so when she missed one of the kicks Trish had passed to her, she thought nothing of it. That is, until Cindy laughed. "Oops!" Alex said with a forced laugh, trying to make light of the situation.

"Oh, she'll never get to play," Cindy said to her friend, just loud enough for both Alex and Trish to hear.

"Ignore them," Trish said.

But Alex's feelings had already been hurt badly enough in the locker room; having Cindy witness her making a mistake was too much to bear. She could feel the tears forming in her eyes.

"Uh-oh," Cindy's friend said loudly. "She's totally going to cry."

Cindy laughed. "Oh man. If she cries about missing a pass, what's she going to do when we're actually playing?" she said. Then she snorted. "Oh. Right. She's not going to get to play."

Alex looked furtively for the coach, but Coach Gregorson was on the other side of the field, giving pointers to another set of girls. Still laughing, Cindy and her friend moved away from Alex and Trish.

The rest of practice was okay—they did a few more exercises with the balls, and then were split up into two teams for a scrimmage. Alex didn't score, but she did feel like she was learning a lot. She couldn't shake the memory of Cindy teasing her, though. For the first time in her entire life, Alex wanted to quit soccer—what was the point if she wasn't going to get to play, and if her teammates were going to be so unfriendly?

Alex had been playing soccer for a long time. At her elementary school, she'd been close friends with all of the girls on her team. So it was strange to be on a team where not only did she not know anyone else, but some girls were mean to her. She was used to a supportive, fun team . . . this was totally different.

Alex and Trish walked to the locker room together after practice. "Try not to get too upset about her," Trish said quietly. "She's just stupid."

Alex sighed. "Yeah, I know," she said. "But it still stinks, getting made fun of."

They reached the school building and Trish pulled the heavy door open. "Just try not to worry, Alex," she said. "And just don't listen to her."

"Okay," Alex said. "I'll try not to let her bother me."

To: BrynnWins
From: SoccerLover
Subject: Soccer Team

Hey, Brynn—
How are you? It's been so long since we talked! I hope school is going well for you——middle school is way different for me. I made the soccer team . . . barely . . . and even though the coach said I wouldn't get to play much this

year, I was really excited to be on the team and to learn enough to be able to play next year.

There's one bad thing, though: this girl Cindy. She and her friends were laughing at me before practice, and I thought maybe I was being paranoid. But then she called me a crybaby while we were practicing. And in the locker room after practice, while I was getting dressed, I heard her say my name. I don't know what she was saying, because she was talking quietly. But it really bothered me. It sounded like she was planning to do something mean. I hope I'm wrong about this.

Other than that, school is okay, I guess. What's up with you? Hope to hear from you soon!

Love,
Alex

To: SoccerLover
From: BrynnWins
Re: Soccer Team

Alex, I am really mad at that girl for making fun of you. I'm sure you're just being paranoid, though. Who would do something really mean just for the sake of it? And if it's really bad you should talk to your coach or something.

Love you. Hope you're feeling better.
B.

chapter SEVEN

Grace> WEDNESDAY

Grace sat down at a chair near the front row of her English classroom and slid her books onto the desk. She smiled sweetly at the girl next to her and opened her pencil case, taking out one freshly sharpened yellow pencil. The girl next to her, Cate, leaned over. "Pop quiz today," she whispered.

"Are you sure?" Grace whispered back.

"Yep. My sister has Roslyn first period, and she told me."

"Thanks," Grace said, biting her lip nervously.

She tried to act confident, but the truth was, she was terrified. Quizzes were hard enough when she was prepared for them!

The bell rang, and Mr. Roslyn walked into the room, shutting the door behind him. As it shut with a loud crack, he strolled toward his desk and picked up a stack of stapled papers. He gave a few to each person who sat in the front row, telling them to pass the quizzes back.

He coughed, and then said, "Okay, class, as I hinted yesterday, here's a quiz about *Hatchet*. Please close your books, take out a pencil, and we'll start when everyone has the quiz." Mr. Roslyn crossed his arms and waited for everyone to prepare for the quiz. Grace watched as he looked around the room. She squeezed her eyes shut, trying desperately to calm herself, and opened them as Mr. Roslyn said, "All right. Now that you're all ready, let's begin."

As she scanned the test, Grace thought she knew the answers to some of the questions for sure, and she was pretty confident about some of the others, but she wasn't positive about any of them. *It's okay*, Grace thought. *I can do this.*

She answered the first couple of questions easily, but then got stuck on an essay question about something that had happened at the beginning of the book. Tapping her pencil against her thigh nervously, Grace tried to remember the answer. After a few minutes of thinking, she gave up, hoping to have time to come back to the question after finishing the rest of the test.

By the time the bell rang, signaling the beginning of lunch, Grace reluctantly brought her quiz to Mr. Roslyn's desk, convinced she'd failed it entirely.

▲ ▲ ▲

Instead of eating in the cafeteria, like she normally would, Grace took her lunch to a quiet corner of the schoolyard so that she could read alone. After the trauma of her pop quiz, she wanted some time to herself. She pulled out her lunch bag and arranged the sandwich, chips, apple, and cranberry juice around her for easy access, and then reached into her backpack for her copy of *The Pinballs*.

As she munched on her lunch, Grace tried to read a few pages of her book. She liked the characters in the story right away, but she was having a hard time paying attention to the plot of the book. After realizing she was reading the same paragraph over and over for almost ten minutes, she shut the book in frustration and simply finished her lunch, staring off into the trees that circled the school.

When she'd eaten everything her mom had packed that morning, Grace shoved the wrappers and apple core back into the lunch bag and walked back into the school toward the cafeteria, where she knew she'd find her friends.

But as she passed Mr. Roslyn's classroom, she stopped in her tracks. Through the small rectangular window set into the wooden door, she could see Mr. Roslyn working at his desk, grading papers while he ate a sandwich.

Grace tentatively walked closer to the door and raised her hand to knock. When she rapped gently at the door, she saw Mr. Roslyn look up. When he saw her, he smiled and motioned for her to come in.

Grace pushed the door open and walked in.

"How can I help you, Miss Matthews?" Mr. Roslyn said, putting down his red pen and pushing the stack of ungraded papers away from him. He shoved his chair back a bit and crossed his arms over his chest.

"Hi, Mr. Roslyn," Grace said. "Um . . . do you have a few minutes to talk?"

Mr. Roslyn uncrossed his arms and gestured to the closest desk. "Of course. Have a seat!"

Grace sat down, placing her backpack carefully

next to her feet. "I wanted to talk to you about reading," she said.

Mr. Roslyn smiled warmly. "One of my favorite things," he said. "But I know not everyone feels that way," he added, leaning back in his chair. "One of the things I've learned as a teacher is that if you really work hard, and really put your mind to it, you'll be able to do anything. Grace, I can already tell you're a fine student, especially when you really put your mind to something. I talked to your parents a few days ago, and they told me you've been studying a lot this year, and that's great. Just keep working at it, and you'll be fine."

"That isn't what's wrong," Grace said quietly.

"Is it that you don't like reading?" Mr. Roslyn prompted.

"No! I like to read!" Grace protested. "I just . . . I've been having some trouble."

Mr. Roslyn frowned. "What's the trouble?" he asked.

"Well," Grace began, looking down at her hands, "I have trouble concentrating. I don't mind reading, but it's hard to get into it." She looked up at her teacher. "Do you ever have a hard time concentrating?" she asked.

"Absolutely, Grace," he replied with a smile. "In fact, when I was your age I had a terrible time reading."

"So what changed?" Grace asked.

Mr. Roslyn frowned thoughtfully. Grace noticed that when he seemed to be thinking, his cheeks turned a bit redder than normal—and they were pretty red to begin with. "Hmmm," he said, still thinking. Then his eyes lit up.

"I know what it was!" he exclaimed. He reached

into his desk drawer and pulled out a tattered book.

"Reading made you like reading?" Grace asked skeptically.

"No," Mr. Roslyn said. "This book made me like reading."

He displayed the book's cover, and Grace gasped. "*Peter Pan?*" she shrieked. "Did you know I was in *Peter Pan* this summer in my camp play?"

Mr. Roslyn smiled widely, displaying rows of sparkling white teeth. "I did not! Who knew there was a thespian among us?"

"Yeah, I played Wendy!" Grace said happily. "So . . . is it your favorite book?"

"No. Not my favorite. But it was once, before I went to college. In college, I read a book called *Ulysses*. Well, in college I read a lot of books, but that one was my favorite ever since. I guess I have a lot of favorites." Mr. Roslyn paused. "Grace, would you like to borrow my copy of *Peter Pan?*"

Grace drew in her breath. "I'd love to!" she exclaimed. "Thanks, Mr. Roslyn!"

"Not as homework, you understand," he cautioned. "For fun." He emphasized the word *fun* by pointing his pencil at Grace.

"Got it, Mr. Roslyn," Grace said. Even though the thought of *extra* reading sounded anything but fun. She forced herself to look enthusiastic. At that moment, the bell rang, signaling the end of the lunch period.

"You hurry along to class. And let me know how you like the book," Mr. Roslyn said. "And try to make a stab at *The Pinballs*, too . . . I think you'll like it more than you think you will."

Grace stood up and slung her backpack around her shoulders. "Thanks, Mr. Roslyn," she said shyly, before heading to the door. Even if she didn't do as well on the quiz as she would have liked, she knew that she'd tried her hardest and that her teacher was on her side.

Posted by: Grace
Subject: Reading

Hi, Lakeview girls! I'm so excited about our book club—I think it's really going to help me in my English class. Plus, my English teacher gave me a copy of *Peter Pan* to read for fun. But I still have to read *Pinballs* for homework. So I think I've heard from everyone about being in the club, except Chelsea. Does anyone know if she's been checking the blog? Chelsea, if you're reading this, let me know if you want to join!

Have you guys ever felt really different from your friends? I have this new friend, Lara, in drama club. She's super smart. She went to this really elite private school. But I really like her a lot, and I know she likes me, too. We hung out last weekend and I want to hang out with her again this weekend. But I feel like when she discovers the truth about me, that I'm not great in school, she won't want to be my friend anymore. Does anyone have any advice?

Anyway, we start *Pinballs* on Monday . . . I plan to have the first chapter read by that day. Hope some of you will, too! I've got to get back to drama club—we're on a break, and I just wanted to say hi!

Love,
Grace

Posted by: Sarah
Re: Reading

You'll love *Peter Pan* (the book), Grace! It's different from the play, but it's still really magical and cool.
Love ya! Sarah

Posted by: Jessie
Re: Reading

Hey, Grace, I have a friend like that, sort of. She's really good at sports, and all of her friends are on the basketball team and stuff. We're best friends because we live in the same neighborhood. We didn't even go to elementary school together. But now that we're in the same middle school, I was really worried that she wouldn't want to be my friend anymore, since we do such different things. You're really lucky to have a friend with the same interests, and I can't imagine that Lara would change her mind about you just because of a couple of bad grades. After all, she likes YOU, right? Not your report card! :) Molly and I are still best friends, even though I'm not the best athlete ever. So I don't think Lara will care. (And if she did, she wouldn't be very cool anyway, right?)
KIT! Jess

▲ ▲ ▲

Natalie> WEDNESDAY

When the bell rang at the end of the school day, Natalie was excited for her skating date with Kyle . . . but totally nervous, too. In fact, she'd been getting more and more jittery all day.

She'd worn her favorite jeans and the red top she'd bought with Hannah, and she knew it was a pretty cute combo. So she wasn't surprised that Kyle blushed when he walked up to her at her locker after school.

"Uh, hey, Nat," he said. He had his rollerblades slung over one shoulder and his backpack over the other. "You ready?"

"Definitely!" Natalie said, trying to make her voice sound steadier than she felt. "Let me just grab my stuff, and I'll be ready to go."

"Awesome," Kyle replied. They walked together through the hallway of the school toward the big entrance doors. Natalie couldn't believe she was on her first real date. *I will remember this date for the rest of my life*, she thought.

Near the entrance, Natalie saw Hannah standing with a couple of other girls. She smiled at her friend, but Hannah just shot her back a strange look. There was no pretending that it was a mistake or something Nat had imagined—obviously Hannah was grouchy that Natalie was going on her date.

Kyle noticed the exchange, and leaned over to Natalie. "That's weird," he said. "Isn't Hannah, like, your best friend?"

"Yeah," Natalie said. *Though these days, I'm not too sure.* She pushed her hair back out of her eyes. "Let's go!" she said, trying to sound more excited. This was her first date, after all, and she wasn't going to let anything ruin it.

Not even losing her best friend.

As Kyle and Natalie walked toward Central Park, they talked about school and about their friends. Kyle told Natalie that over the summer he'd started hanging out with kids from his neighborhood instead of just friends from school. "That's cool," Nat said. "I made a lot of friends this summer."

"Really? At camp?" Kyle asked, surprised.

Natalie laughed. "Why do you sound so shocked? I spent eight weeks living in a tiny cabin with a bunch of other girls. Obviously we'd be friends."

Kyle blushed. "Well, right," he said. "I guess I'm just surprised because, you know, um, I remember you weren't too excited about camp when you first told me about it."

"No, I wasn't," Natalie said. She smiled, remembering the first few days at camp, when she'd hated getting up early, hated being all sweaty, and hated being out in nature. But she'd grown to really love Camp Lakeview. "I mean, yeah, I missed New York. But . . . I don't know. I guess eleven-year-old girls have more in common than you'd think, no matter where they're from."

"And eleven-year-old boys," Kyle said quietly.

Natalie knew he was talking about Simon. Simon who had finally called her the other night and left a message—though they'd been playing phone tag and still hadn't spoken. But what could she say to make Kyle feel better? She did like Simon—and she liked Kyle, too. *Boys,* she thought. *Are they really worth it?*

They reached the bottom of Central Park at 59th Street. Kyle shaded his eyes against the sun and looked for a bench where they could put their Rollerblades on. "Hey, over here," he said.

"Do you want to get a Frappuccino first?" Natalie

asked, looking longingly at a Starbucks across the avenue.

"Uh . . . not really," Kyle said. "I don't like coffee." He started across the street toward the bench.

"Okay . . ." Natalie mumbled, surprised. Even if Kyle wasn't into caffeine, wouldn't it have been polite to take her anyway? *Well, I'm new to this dating thing*, she thought, deciding to be a good sport. She hoisted her backpack and followed Kyle across the street.

They sat on a stone bench and changed into their Rollerblades, shoving their shoes into their bags. Then they started skating slowly through the park, winding their way along the paths. Natalie loved Central Park, especially in the early autumn, when the grass was bright green, the sky was a brilliant blue, the trees were just beginning to change colors, and everyone in the park seemed to be in a great mood as they lounged on blankets, Rollerbladed or ran, pushed baby strollers, and played with dogs. It was Hannah and Natalie's favorite place to come, any time of the year, but especially during the first month of school. For as long as Nat could remember, they'd made a point of coming to the park a few times a week. When they were young, they'd come with their mothers, but now, they'd go alone. And they'd always get a Frappuccino, or ice cream, or lemonade. It wasn't that Natalie minded being there without Hannah, and with Kyle. She just wished that Hannah wasn't mad at her.

In fact, Hannah being mad at her was enough to put Natalie in a bad mood. *I can't believe this*, she thought. *I've been looking forward to my first date for, like, my whole life.* She decided to put on a happy face. "So, Kyle," she said. "What did you do this summer?"

"Oh, you know, that acting school," he said, turning to look at Nat.

"Right, duh," Natalie replied. "Was it fun?"

"Yeah, it was really fun. I learned a lot."

"Cool," Nat said.

"So, you had a boyfriend this summer, huh?" Kyle asked quietly.

Natalie whipped her head to look at him. "What?"

"Simon, or whatever. The guy Hannah was talking about."

"He wasn't my boyfriend."

"Oh. Okay. Do you still talk to him?" Natalie thought she heard a little jealousy in Kyle's voice.

"I haven't talked to him since camp," she said honestly. But she felt slightly annoyed that she was being forced to defend herself.

"Oh, cool," Kyle replied, looking visibly less nervous.

They skated in semi-silence for a half an hour or so. And for the first time in her life, Natalie found herself not able to think of anything to say. *Quick, Nat, come up with something*, she thought. *Anything. TV, sports, school. . . .* But she couldn't think of a thing. She didn't know what the problem was, whether it was Kyle talking about Simon, or feeling bad about Hannah. *I guess this Hannah thing is bothering me more than I expected*, she admitted to herself. *Or maybe dating's just harder than I expected!* She remembered, though, that she and Simon had never had trouble coming up with things to talk about at camp. Could it be that Natalie and Simon just had more . . . chemistry? Whatever that meant, anyway.

She noticed that they had skated in several loops to end up near the opening to 79th Street. "Hey, Kyle?" Natalie said tentatively. "I think I should head home."

Kyle looked taken aback. "Oh . . . okay," he said. "Um . . . do you feel sick or something?"

She checked her watch—it was only four thirty. "I . . . uh . . . promised my mom I'd be home by five," she lied, crossing her fingers behind her back. "And it'll take me a little while to get there," she added for good measure.

"Okay," Kyle said. He looked at the ground. "Thanks for hanging out, Nat," he said. "I had a really good time."

"Me too!" Natalie said, forcing a smile.

I did have a good time, she thought, as she skated down 79th Street toward Broadway. *But I just want to get home.* She was already looking forward to maybe ordering in some Thai food and relaxing on the couch in front of a good Hilary Duff DVD . . . and not thinking about friends or boys or about growing up. Just being Natalie. Wasn't that perfectly okay?

To: Alyssa11
From: NatalieNYC
Subject: Boys, etc . . . .

hey, alyssa. so, today i went on a date with kyle (you remember, i talked about him at camp). it was okay. i mean, it was fun——we went rollerblading in central park. but he's not as cool as simon was. he didn't want to stop and get frappuccinos . . . and i don't know. it just wasn't what i expected. he's a fun guy, but . . . he kept asking me about simon. and i just didn't feel like explaining anything. we didn't have that much to say to each other. sort of a letdown.

i guess part of the problem is my friend hannah. she's

been really weird since i got back from camp. saying things about me having boyfriends, and just acting generally un-hannah-like. and the other day, when i was going off on my date with kyle, hannah got really awkward about it. it really put me in a terrible mood.

i'm having a good time in middle school, but i feel like everything's different. hannah's different, or else she just thinks i am, and instead of just hanging out with someone, you have to be their girlfriend. it's too much pressure. it makes me want to curl up in my room——with some fashion magazines, of course——and not come out till high school.

the thing is, hannah thinks i shouldn't have a boyfriend, much less two boyfriends. but i don't! i really like simon, and i like kyle——or, I did before today——but i'm not planning my wedding or anything. why can't i hang out with both of them?

what should i do? should i call simon back? or should i just forget about boys altogether? and should i talk to hannah, or just let her get over it? AHHHH! i wish this was easier. who knew middle school would cause so many problems??

i'd better go——my mom just got home. i'm going to convince her to order in thai food.

luv, nat

chapter EIGHT

Alex> WEDNESDAY

Alex had never been so pumped in her life. It was the final moments of their first soccer game, and the Rockets were up by four points, meaning they'd definitely beat the Chargers. She couldn't believe it, but she was so into the game that it almost didn't matter that she wasn't actually playing. Almost.

The minute the thought had popped into her brain, everything changed.

"Okay, Alex, you're going in for Carla," the coach said.

At first, Alex thought she'd heard wrong. "Seriously?" she asked excitedly. Her stomach did back flips. She was nervous, but she couldn't wait to get out on the field. After looking up into the stands and giving her mom a thumbs-up, she checked to make sure that her hair was tightly in place and that her shoelaces were tied. The coach blew her whistle to signal a time-out. Coach Gregorson motioned for Carla to come off the field, and Carla ran off.

She and Alex high-fived as Alex ran onto the field. Once the coach blew her whistle again, the game was back on. Alex was afraid her knees were going to buckle beneath her, but as her feet found the ball, her confidence returned. Soccer was as natural to Alex as breathing. Suddenly, Alex found herself kicking the ball down the field, weaving through her opponents until she was directly in front of the goal, unguarded. *Yes!* she thought. There was no doubt in her mind: She was going to make this goal.

Everyone in the stands was cheering and whistling, but Alex blocked out all the noise as she made for the goal. She raised her right foot to kick the ball into the goal, watching only the opposing team's goalie and waiting for the perfect moment. She lowered her foot toward the ball, readied herself, and . . .

Suddenly found herself on her back, with her ankle twisted in excruciating, red-hot pain. For a minute, she couldn't figure out what had happened, and then Alex realized she'd been tripped. She looked up and saw Cindy standing there, a terrified look on her face. "Oh, man," Cindy said. "Oh no. Are you okay?" The cheering in the stands turned to worried silence, and the referee blew his whistle, stopping the game.

Alex couldn't believe what had just happened. "Did you trip me?" she whispered incredulously.

"No!" Cindy said, backing away. "I didn't mean to, I swear, I swear Alex, I'd never do that."

"What happened?" Coach Gregorson asked, standing above Alex. She bent down. "Are you all right, Alex?" she asked softly.

"I'm okay. Cindy—I don't know what happened, but I was about to kick the ball and then I was on the ground," Alex replied. Her chin trembled. "My leg really, really hurts."

The coach looked to the sidelines, motioning for the school nurse to come to the field. As the nurse made her way to the field, Coach asked, "Cindy, what happened?"

"I was just coming up behind her to help," Cindy said plaintively. "She slowed down and I didn't realize it, and all of a sudden I was right behind her, and as she lowered her foot I just—"

"Okay," Coach said. "I'm sure it was an accident. Regardless, it looks to me like Alex has sprained her ankle. Alex, is your mom here?"

Alex sat up a bit and looked toward the bleachers, shading her eyes. "Yes," she said. "The lady with the brown hair by the bottom of the bleachers." She looked up to see that her mother was already on her way down, a nervous expression on her face.

Nurse Clain, breathless and red-faced from hurrying onto the field, arrived and kneeled down beside Alex. She picked up Alex's foot, asking, "Does this hurt?"

Alex nodded her head. "It doesn't feel broken. I broke my ankle once and it wasn't like this."

"I think it's just a sprain," the nurse said comfortingly. "If it was a break, you'd be in agonizing pain right now."

Alex's mom ran up then and crouched down. "Honey, are you okay?" she asked, her eyebrows knit together in a worried frown.

"My leg hurts," Alex replied. She bit her lip as tears started to sting her eyes. "It hurts a lot," she went on, the tears that had been threatening to fall finally making their way down her face. "But I can move it, a little."

"Good," Nurse Clain responded. She pulled a tissue out of her pocket and leaned over to wipe the tears from Alex's face. "I'm sure it's just a sprain, but let's take you to the emergency room to find out."

"I'll go pull around the car," Alex's mom said.

"Great. We're going to help you up, Alex," Coach said. "Put your arms around our shoulders, and try to hop on your other foot."

Alex sat up and looked at Cindy. The older girl looked petrified, her face ghost white. She clenched her hands to her mouth as the coach and the nurse reached down to help Alex to her feet.

As she hopped off the field, the onlookers rose to their feet and clapped for her.

"Alex," Coach Gregorson said, as they headed toward the parking lot, "you were great out there." Alex gingerly got into the passenger seat of her mom's red station wagon. "I'm really impressed. I think you may be playing more this year than any of us thought you would."

"Really?" Alex replied. "Thanks, Coach!"

Her leg throbbed and her face was still wet and tear-stained, but Alex didn't care. Even though she got hurt, she had definitely kicked butt on the field that afternoon. She had proven her worth to her coach—and to herself!

The nurse was right: It was just a sprain, much to Alex's relief. When she and her mom got home from the hospital, her mom set her up in a comfortable chair in the living room, put in a DVD of Alex's favorite movie, and handed her the remote. "I'll make you dinner," she said, tucking a comfortable, multicolored blanket around Alex. "What do you want? Anything at all."

Alex thought for a minute. "Um . . . how about chicken stir-fry?" she said.

"Okay, honey. Sit tight."

Alex started watching the movie, and when dinner was ready, her mom sat down in the living room to watch with her.

The phone rang, and Alex's mom went to pick it up. "Hello?" she said. "Al, it's for you—it's Bridgette."

"Really?" Alex asked. "Uh . . . okay." She hadn't even seen Bridgette at school that day, except for in math, where they hadn't had time to talk. Bridgette took gymnastics after school and therefore couldn't come to Alex's game. Her mom handed her the cordless phone and walked back toward the kitchen.

"Hi, Bridgette," Alex said tentatively.

"Hey, Al," Bridgette replied, a note of concern in her voice. "I heard about what happened during the soccer game! Are you okay?"

"Yes," Alex said, reaching for the remote to pause the movie. "I just sprained my ankle. It hurts, but it's okay."

"What happened?" Bridgette asked.

Alex shifted in her chair. "Well, I was about to score a goal and all of a sudden this girl, Cindy, came up behind me and I guess she didn't realize I was slowing down to kick, and she accidentally tripped me."

She heard Bridgette draw her breath in sharply. "Oh, Alex, good thing you're okay!"

"I know. It wouldn't be so bad except that at first I was positive Cindy did it on purpose. The other day she made fun of me for wearing my hair in pigtails, and then when I messed up a pass she laughed at me again. So when it happened today . . ."

"I'm sure she didn't do it on purpose. I mean, I know she's been not so nice to you, but that would be awful," Bridgette agreed.

"Yeah, I hope it was just an accident." Alex sighed. "It's funny, if that happened last year I wouldn't even have wondered for a minute if it was on purpose. If I got hurt, and a girl on my team had done it, I would know for sure that she hadn't done it on purpose. I guess it's just another thing that stinks about middle school."

Bridgette was quiet for a moment. "You don't like middle school?" she asked.

Alex paused before answering. *It's time for me to be honest with Bridgette,* she decided. *If she's really my best friend, she'll understand.* "No!" Alex finally replied, emphatically. "I hate it. I don't know anybody, there's way more homework, you have to try out for soccer, people are mean . . ." She stopped.

"But it isn't only bad, Alex," Bridgette said gently. "I mean, we have better classes, way more freedom, we can use pens . . ." She and Alex laughed in unison. "And that's not all," Bridgette went on. "It's hard right now because it's, like, totally different. But it'll be awesome once we have tons of new friends and stuff."

Alex bit her lip. "But you're the one meeting people," she said, shifting the phone to her other ear. "Not me. I'm just boring."

Bridgette laughed. "Alex, don't be ridiculous! You're my best friend! You'll meet people with me! I'm not going to go to any parties without you, or anything . . . and I'm not leaving you behind. We're in this together! Besides, it's not like you don't have your own thing going on—what about soccer, after all? I mean, other than Cindy, of course."

"But I never see you anymore," Alex said quietly.

"That's just because I've had a lot of homework, and we don't have classes together, really," Bridgette reassured her. "Don't worry. You'll always be my best friend, Alex."

Alex sighed with relief. "Well, that makes middle school a bit easier, I guess," she said. "Hey, maybe I'll meet people since I'll be limping around school all week!"

Bridgette laughed. "I'd better go," she said. "My mom's calling me for dinner."

"Okay," Alex replied. "See you tomorrow." After they hung up, she couldn't believe how much better she felt after talking to Bridgette. Having a best friend definitely made most things easier, at least.

Natalie> THURSDAY

In school on Thursday morning, Natalie couldn't help but notice that conversations seemed to stop the minute she passed by people in the hall, and that when she walked by, most people's eyes were following her. After an entire morning of weirdness, she finally leaned over to a classmate, Chloe, and said, "Okay, so, why am I suddenly such a celebrity?"

Chloe laughed. "Are you kidding?" she asked. "It's you and Kyle. Everyone's totally obsessed with how you two are a couple."

Natalie was taken aback. "What?" she asked incredulously. "I'm not Kyle's girlfriend. We went skating. That's it."

Chloe shrugged. "Well, that's not what he's telling people," she said. "I heard that you guys went out yesterday, and now you're his girlfriend."

"Well, it's not true," Natalie said. She slumped into her chair. "I mean, I like him, but we just went Rollerblading. It's not like we're married or anything."

Hannah walked into the class and sat down far away from Natalie. Nat turned in her chair to look at her friend, but Hannah pointedly avoided Nat's gaze and opened up her notebook. She began writing in it, and Natalie turned back around.

"What's up with you and Hannah?" Chloe asked. "Aren't you guys best friends anymore?"

"I thought we were," Natalie said. She sighed.

Everything was wrong! Her best friend was not her friend at all, and a boy she'd hung out with, like, once was suddenly her boyfriend. Things were as complicated as ever, and Nat didn't like it. Not one bit.

▲ ▲ ▲

After class, Natalie rushed out of the room before anyone could ask her questions about her "date" with Kyle. She headed to the locker bay and was intercepted by Kyle himself.

"Hey, Nat," he said, walking alongside her to the lockers.

"Hi, Kyle," Natalie said, embarrassed.

"How's it going?"

"Good," Natalie replied, forcing a smile.

"So . . . what are you doing after school?" Kyle asked. They reached Natalie's locker, and he reached out to take her books as she twirled the combination lock to open her locker.

"It's okay, I can carry them," she said. "Um . . . I don't know what I'm doing. My mom told me to come right home."

"Oh," Kyle said, sounding disappointed. "I was thinking we could go to Central Park again."

"Well, I don't have my Rollerblades or anything," Natalie replied. She put her books into her locker and took out the one she needed for her English class second period.

"That's okay," Kyle said quickly. "We could just walk around. We could even go to Starbucks."

"I can't today," Natalie said. "I'm sorry."

"Oh. Okay," he replied. He was obviously disappointed.

"I'd better get to class," Natalie said, slamming her locker and rushing off before he could say anything or offer to carry her books for her. As she left, she was aware of him standing there and watching her.

Natalie felt bad. Kyle was really nice—she especially appreciated that he wanted to take her to Starbucks—but she'd finally talked to Simon last night and they'd had a great conversation. No one made her laugh the way Simon did. If Kyle was looking for a girl-friend, well, then she just wasn't ready.

At lunch, Natalie scanned the cafeteria for Hannah, who was sitting alone at a corner table. She hurried across the room and put her lunch bag down onto Hannah's table. Hannah looked up at her and began to pick up her things, as if to leave, but Natalie sat down and said, "Hannah, please don't leave. Please let me talk to you."

"Don't you want to sit with your boyfriend?" Hannah asked snidely.

"He's not my boyfriend, Han," Natalie said, frustrated. "And even if he were, you're my best friend, and I want to work this out."

"That's not what he said," Hannah replied. "I heard all about it first period."

"I know," Natalie said forcefully. "But it's not true. I am not his girlfriend, and he is not my boyfriend. Look, this boyfriend stuff is pretty heavy. I really like Kyle, but I can still carry my own books to class, and I can still sit with my best friend at lunch."

Hannah softened. "Oh," she said quietly. "I just assumed . . ."

"Well, you assumed wrong," Natalie cut in. "We just went Rollerblading for, like, an hour. He didn't even want to get a Frappuccino beforehand! It was fun, but I wished the whole time that I was Rollerblading with you, instead." She smiled at Hannah. "I really miss you, Han," she went on softly. She opened her lunch bag and took out her sandwich, slowly unwrapping the plastic.

Hannah sighed. "I miss you too, Nat. I just feel like you're into things I'm not into right now."

"Hannah, that's ridiculous!" Natalie cried, putting down her sandwich.

"No, it's not," Hannah said. She sipped her soda. "I don't like boys, and I don't care about makeup and stuff. Sushi and shopping, sure. But not boys. Not yet." Hannah looked down at her open bag of chips. "I just feel like you're growing up way faster than I am, and I don't want to be your boring, babyish friend."

"I'm not growing up faster than you," Natalie protested. "I happened to meet a couple of boys that I was interested in. It isn't anything drastic. And besides—I've always been into makeup!"

Hannah opened her bag and drew out an apple, which she polished gently on her T-shirt. "It seems like a really big difference."

"Just because our lives might be a little different right now—it doesn't change anything," Natalie said. She thought for a moment. "I mean, our lives have always been different. That's one of the greatest things about our friendship!"

"I know," Hannah replied.

"I mean, I've been a little self-absorbed," Natalie admitted.

"And I've been a little jealous," Hannah said quietly. "It is pretty stupid, huh?"

"Absolutely." Natalie bit into her cheese sandwich and then took a sip of her soda. "But you should know—all of this boy stuff? Just makes me need you as my friend more than ever! Seriously, I'm so confused, and you're the one who keeps me sane."

"Barely," Hannah quipped dryly.

"Fine, point taken," Nat conceded. "Do you want to go Rollerblading after school?"

"I'd love to go Rollerblading," Hannah said excitedly.

"On one condition, though," Natalie said in her best serious voice.

"What?" Hannah said, frowning.

"Frappuccinos first," Nat said, winking.

To: Alyssa11
From: NatalieNYC
Subject: Hannah, boys . . .

hey, alyssa——i just wanted to write and thank you for your advice about hannah. i talked to her today, and we managed to figure things out. i think she was just feeling, like, with all this boy stuff going on, i didn't need her anymore. but i pointed out that that's exactly why i need her now, more than ever! i mean, kyle and i hung out one time, and all of a sudden i'm his girlfriend? no way. especially 'cause of how simon and i have been having these great phone conversations and text messages and stuff. i just started getting into boys——i'm not looking for anything serious. so it's good to have hannah to help me deal.

anyway, just wanted to let you know how much your advice helped. hope everything is okay with you. write soon and let me know what's up!

luv, nat

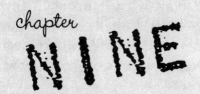

chapter
NINE

Alex⟩ THURSDAY

"Bye, honey," Alex's mom said, kissing her on the forehead.

"See you after practice, Mom," Alex replied. She shifted her backpack onto her back, picked up her crutches, and started slowly hopping toward the entrance to her school building. She was aware of the looks she was getting from everyone as she hobbled in, but none of the looks were mean.

A boy she didn't recognize held the front door open for her.

"Wow, I heard about what happened, but I didn't know you'd have to be on crutches!" he said, waiting until Alex had fully made it through the door before following behind her toward the lockers.

"Yeah, it's just for a couple of weeks, so I don't strain it," Alex said. She couldn't believe the boy—who she thought was probably an eighth-grader—knew who she was.

"Man, I was talking to Cindy this morning. She feels so bad about what happened," the boy went on. "She was like, 'Peter, I totally didn't mean to do it!'"

"Well, I would hope she didn't mean to do it," Alex said, glad to learn the boy's name. "Why would anyone do that on purpose?"

Peter shrugged. "Cindy can be a little snotty sometimes, but she'd never hurt someone like that. Do you need help with your backpack or anything?" He stopped with Alex in front of her locker.

Alex smiled. "No, I'm okay," she said. "Thanks, though!"

"No problem. Maybe I'll see you at lunch or something. Are you going to the football game on Friday?" Peter asked.

"I don't know. Maybe!" Alex said. "See you later!"

"Bye," Peter said, smiling.

Alex opened her locker and gingerly set her crutches to one side. She placed her backpack inside, and took out her book for first period. As she was reaching onto the top shelf for a notebook and a pen, Bridgette came up next to her.

"Hey, Al!" she said. "Oh my gosh, you didn't tell me you had to get crutches!"

Alex swung her locker door shut. "Yeah, just for a couple of weeks," she said. "They aren't so bad . . . it's kind of fun, actually."

Bridgette leaned in closer. In a conspiratorial tone, she whispered, "So . . . I saw you talking to Peter!"

Alex laughed and shrugged her shoulders. "I didn't know you knew him—but yeah, he held the door for me and then walked me to my locker. Are you friends with him?"

"No, but I know who he is. He's like one of the cutest boys in the eighth grade!" Bridgette exclaimed. "What did he say to you?" She reached for Alex's book. "Let me help you," she added.

Alex swung herself onto her crutches. "Thanks," she said. "Well, he told me he heard about what happened, and then he asked if I was going to the football game on Friday."

"What did you say?" Bridgette responded excitedly as they made their way toward Alex's homeroom.

"I told him I didn't know," Alex said, laughing. "Do you want to go?"

"Absolutely!" Bridgette said. "It'll be really fun!"

They reached Alex's classroom, and Bridgette followed her in, placing Alex's books on an empty desk for her. "See you at lunch," she said.

"See you!" Alex replied. She settled herself into the chair and opened her book.

Lucy walked into the classroom and slid into a chair next to Alex. "Alex, I heard about what happened!" she said. "Are you okay?"

"Yeah, I'm fine," Alex said, placing her finger into the book so she wouldn't lose her page. "I just have to use these crutches for a while."

"Oh, wow," Lucy said. "Gosh, I heard last night, and I wanted to call you, but I didn't have your phone number!"

"I should give it to you," Alex said. "Then we could hang out over the weekend."

"Definitely!" Lucy replied happily. "So, are you going to be able to play soccer anymore?"

"Oh, yeah," Alex said. "I can't play for a couple of weeks, but I'm still going to go to practice. I'll be able to learn some stuff from watching."

"That's good," Lucy replied just as their teacher walked into the room. She went on in a whisper, "We'll talk more later, okay?" Alex nodded and opened her book again.

By the time lunch rolled around, a dozen people—mostly strangers, or kids she barely knew from class—had come up to talk to Alex about what had happened. One girl told her that Cindy had cried about it after the game, which made Alex feel better. She hadn't wanted to believe that Cindy would have hurt her on purpose, but the mean comments Cindy had made about her made it difficult to think that the injury had been an accident. So it was good to know that she hadn't meant to hurt Alex. Not that Alex really wanted anyone to *cry*, but still.

At lunch, as soon as Alex entered the cafeteria, she heard Bridgette calling to her. As she hobbled across the room, careful not to slide on the hard linoleum floor, she passed Peter, who was sitting at a table with his friends. "Hey, Alex," he said casually. "How's it going?"

Alex beamed at him. "Great! The crutches aren't so bad." She stopped walking. "Once you get used to them, I mean."

"Man, I was on crutches one time," one of Peter's friends said. "I broke my leg. The worst part was, it was summer, so I couldn't go swimming."

Peter laughed. "Dude, you can't swim anyway," he said.

The other boy shrugged. "That's true, but maybe if I could've that summer, I would've learned!"

"So did you decide if you're coming to the football game?" Peter asked Alex.

"I think my friend Bridgette and I are going," Alex replied.

"Cool!" Peter said. "See you tomorrow night then."

"See you," Alex said, beginning to walk toward Bridgette's table.

She set the crutches at an angle against the table and sat down before realizing she hadn't gotten any food. "You want me to grab you some lunch?" Bridgette asked.

"That would be amazing," Alex replied with a smile. "Thanks, Bridgette." She handed Bridgette a few crumpled dollar bills she'd had clenched in her hand, and Bridgette hopped up and went to the hot lunch line.

The two girls gossiped and laughed while they ate, and when the bell rang to signal the end of lunch, Bridgette cleared Alex's plate for her, and helped her get to her locker.

"See you in math!" Bridgette said before leaving to get her own books.

"Bye!" Alex said. It was funny—she knew that hurting her ankle had made her kind of a celebrity, but she didn't mind, because it gave her the opportunity to talk to people she might have been too shy to approach. Talk about finding a silver lining!

Posted by: Alex
Subject: My hurt ankle!

Hi, guys—

I've started reading *The Pinballs*! It's so good. I hope you all like it so far!

Also, I sprained my ankle yesterday during my soccer game——and because of it, I didn't make the goal I would've scored! It's okay, though. It isn't a bad sprain, and I only have to be on crutches for a couple of weeks. And for some reason, being on crutches makes me a semi-celebrity in school! Lots of people I don't even know are coming up to me to talk to me about my injury. Isn't that crazy? Who would have thought it would take something like this to help me meet new friends?

Anyway, no one has posted in a couple of days, so I thought I would write. What's everyone up to?

Love, Al

grace> THURSDAY

After drama club, Grace let the front door slam behind her as she placed her backpack on the floor and began taking off her sneakers. She didn't expect anyone to be at home, so she jumped when her mother called from the kitchen, "Grace? Can you please come in here?"

"Uh . . . okay, Mom, I'm just taking my shoes off," she called. She placed her sneakers side by side under the coat rack and walked slowly to the kitchen.

Her parents sat beside each other at the kitchen table. "Hey, guys," she said nervously. "What's up? Why are you home so early?"

"We need to talk, Grace," her father said. He

motioned to the chair across the table from them. "Sit down, please."

Grace gingerly slid the chair out and sat down. She bit her nails. "Um . . . is everything okay?"

Grace's parents looked at each other. "No, everything is not okay," Grace's mother said. "We talked to Mr. Roslyn today."

"Oh!" Grace said. "Did he tell you that he lent me *Peter Pan* to read? For fun, not for schoolwork. And I told him that I was in the play, and—"

"He called to tell us how proud he was of the progress you've been making," Grace's dad said. "And we were really proud too. We heard you got a B on your pop quiz, and he told us about you coming to him for help, which must have been hard for you to do."

Grace nodded. "He was really nice," she said.

"Right. He's a nice man," Grace's dad went on. "We also told him how you were spending afternoons at the library."

Grace's heart sunk. "You did?" she asked quietly.

"Funny, Grace, you never told us he was the after-school library monitor," Grace's mom interjected.

"He is?" Grace said, for lack of anything better to say. She thought about making one of her patented dramatic gestures, but then thought better of it.

"He is. Which is why he sounded surprised when we mentioned your after-school studying," Grace's father said. He crossed his arms and looked at Grace's mother. "He asked if perhaps we meant the public library."

Grace looked down at her hands, folded in her lap. "Oh," she said quietly.

"Grace, what have you been doing after school?" her mother asked.

Grace looked at her. "I . . ." She paused. She knew that she was about to get grounded—she could tell by the look on her parents' faces. She sighed. "I joined the drama club. It meets every day after school. I've been having a great time—"

"Grace, I can't believe you'd join the drama club after we specifically told you that you needed to work on your grades this year!" her father said angrily. Grace's heart sank. There went any chance she had to convince them that she could handle drama club. Now even straight A's wouldn't matter.

"And I can't believe," her mother put in, "that I've been so proud of you, for how hard you're working, and for the effort I thought you were making."

Grace felt tears build up in her eyes. "I have been working hard, Mom," she said. "I have been making an effort. I read all of *Hatchet* and I got a B on the quiz, and my friends from camp are going to do the book club with me again for our next book, which is *The Pinballs*, and I started reading it early, and I talked to Mr. Roslyn . . ."

She stopped, closing her eyes against the sting of the tears. She could tell her hard work wasn't going to make a difference in the face of the lies she'd told. "I'm really sorry," she finished quietly, opening her eyes again. "I thought I could do both, be a good student and be in the drama club. I really love drama club. I made a bunch of new friends, and . . ." She trailed off as a single tear spilled out of her eye.

"Grace," her mother said softly, "you are grounded.

For one week. And I'm going to call the drama club leader and tell her that you are not allowed to participate any longer. You will come home immediately from school and do your homework."

"But Mom, all of my friends are in drama club," Grace begged. "Please don't make me quit. I'm doing so well in it, and I'm doing my homework, and . . . please don't make me quit drama club. Please."

Grace's father shook his head. "No, Grace. We told you from the beginning you wouldn't be allowed to be in drama club. We thought you'd appreciate being allowed to join after the semester, if you maintained a B average. You've really disappointed us, and so that offer is gone. You will quit drama club."

"But—" Grace began.

Her father held up his hand. "Stop, Grace," he said. "Our answer is final."

"Okay," Grace said sadly. She looked at her parents. "May I please be excused?" she asked.

"Don't you want dinner?" her mom asked. "I made spaghetti."

"No," Grace said. "I'll eat some later."

Grace's mom sighed. "Then yes, you can be excused, Grace. I'm sorry about all this."

"I'm sorry, Mom," Grace said. Tears began streaming ever faster down her face, and she turned and ran to the staircase, pausing only slightly to grab her backpack. In her room, she threw herself onto her bed and sobbed.

After her tears had subsided slightly, she sat up, wiped her face with her sleeve, and walked to the computer desk. She immediately went to the Camp Lakeview blog. There was a new message from Alex, which she read and responded to quickly. After she'd read Alex's message, she checked her e-mail. There was one new e-mail, from their camp counselor, Julie. The subject was "URGENT ACTION NEEDED!" so Grace clicked on it right away. After reading it, her problems didn't seem so big anymore.

From: CounselorJulie
Subject: URGENT ACTION NEEDED!

Hi, girls——
I got some terrible news today. Chelsea's mom e-mailed me, saying that Chelsea's dad is sick.
She didn't tell me what was wrong, but I got the impression it's not good. Her parents told her the news right when she returned home from camp. That's why we haven't heard from her at all on the blog.
Anyway, it would be really nice if we could do something to let her know that we're thinking of her. I know it would make her feel better.
Hope you guys are all okay.
Love,
Julie

Grace immediately sent an e-mail to all the camp girls.

From: Grrrrace
Re: URGENT ACTION NEEDED!

You guys . . . we have to do something.
XO
Grace

chapter
TEN

Jenna> FRIDAY

Lying in her bed, Jenna coughed loudly. She checked the clock: seven forty-five. She should have been downstairs ready to leave for school five minutes earlier.

She heard footsteps on the stairs, and there was a knock on her door. "Jenna?" her mom called. "You in there? It's about time to leave for school," she said.

"Uhhh . . ." Jenna groaned.

The door to her bedroom creaked open. "Oh, Jenna . . ." her mom said sympathetically. "That cold you've been fighting all week seems to have caught up with you, huh?"

"I guess so," Jenna answered in her best sick voice.

Her mom put her hand on Jenna's forehead. "You do feel a little warm. . . . Okay, honey. You should stay home today to rest. I have to go to work, but I'll bring up some juice for you, and I'll send a note to school with Adam."

"Thanks, Mom," Jenna croaked. "I think I'm just going to stay in bed all day."

"I'll bring home some soup for you on my lunch break, sweetheart."

"Okay," Jenna said, rolling over onto her stomach. "Bye, Mom."

"Bye, sweetheart," her mom said. "Feel better."

She left, and Jenna waited until she heard the front door slam and her mom's car pull out of the driveway before she got up and headed into the family room to watch TV.

At about nine thirty, just as second period was ending, she got a call from Nicole. "I can't talk long," her friend said. "I have to run to class. But are you really sick, or are you faking?"

"What do you think?" Jenna asked.

"Wow, your mom believed you?" Nicole asked.

"Yeah, she totally bought it," Jenna said. "I coughed a lot, and used the ol' warm-washcloth-on-the-forehead trick. You know, where you put it on your forehead, and then dry off your face, so it's still warm? It was perfect timing, too—she came in like three seconds after I got back into bed."

"Nice," Nicole replied. "Well, you'd better have a miracle recovery. The party's going to be tonight, instead of tomorrow."

Jenna's heart sank. "What? Why?" she asked.

"My parents are having a party tomorrow night," Nicole said. "So they told me I couldn't have my friends over at the same time."

"Oh no!" Jenna responded. "Mom'll never let me go!"

"Well, start working on it," Nicole said. "You'll work it out. Maybe when she gets home from work you could act like you feel better, or something."

"No, that won't work, because then I'll have to go to my dad's!" Jenna replied.

"Oh. Right. I forgot," Nicole said. She paused. "Man. I wish I could think of something. I'll let you know if I do. But now I'd better go—the bell's about to ring. See you later!"

"Bye," Jenna said weakly. She hung up the phone and stared blankly at the receiver for a moment. What was she going to do? She had to come up with a plan . . . and fast. No way would her mom let her go to Nicole's party if she was sick . . . and no way could she stay home from her dad's house if she wasn't sick. She had a real problem.

When her mom came home at lunch, she'd decided what to do. Instead of watching talk shows, game shows, and soap operas all day, Jenna had been lying in her bed and thinking about the problem at hand. Once she remembered that her mom had planned on driving all four kids to their dad's house, she had it all figured out.

Jenna's mom walked into the house carrying a take-out container of soup. After setting it down on the kitchen table, she climbed the stairs to Jenna's room and opened the door.

"Hey, Jen," she said, sitting down on Jenna's bed. "Are you feeling any better?"

"No," Jenna replied, rolling over to face her mom. "You're going to stay with me tonight, right?"

Jenna's mom looked worried. "Well, I promised your dad I'd drive you guys to his house," she said. "And I have to run some errands, too. You'll obviously stay home, but you'll be alone for a few hours."

Jenna bit her lip. "Oh," she said. "Okay. What time are you going to leave?"

"Matt has science club after school, so we'll probably leave after dinner," Jenna's mom said. "At about seven or so. But I'll be home before ten for sure, honey," she added quickly.

"Okay, Mom," Jenna said.

Her mom checked her watch. "I'd better get back to work, but I put your soup on the kitchen table. Do you want me to bring it up for you?"

"No, that's okay, Mom," Jenna replied. "I'll go down and eat it in a while."

"All right, sweetie," Jenna's mom said, leaning over and kissing her on the forehead. "Feel better. You feel a bit cooler already."

"Bye, Mom," Jenna said, closing her eyes and rolling over again.

"Bye, honey," her mom said, getting up and closing the door behind her.

The phone rang about fifteen minutes later, and Jenna leapt out of bed to answer it. "Hey, Jen," Nicole said. "Did you figure stuff out?"

"Yeah! I forgot that my mom is driving Matt, Steph, and Adam to my dad's. She said she had some other stuff to do, too—which means that for a few hours, at least, I can come over!"

"Yay!" Nicole said. "I have to go to lunch, but I'll see you tonight! What time can you come over?"

"I think seven or so," Jenna replied. "See you then!"

"Bye!" Nicole said.

Jenna hung up the phone and traipsed down the stairs to the kitchen. She took the lid off her chicken noodle soup and dunked in the plastic spoon her mom had laid on top of the container. She was in a great mood—she couldn't wait till Nicole's party!

After eating, she decided to pick out what to wear. She dug through her closet for the better part of an hour, finally settling on a cute denim skirt and a yellow shirt that had a butterfly printed on the front. She checked her digital clock—it was only one fifteen. Six hours till party time . . .

▲ ▲ ▲

grace > FRIDAY

Grace was on her way home from school when Lara caught up with her.

"Aren't you coming to drama tonight?" Lara asked breathlessly.

"No," Grace replied sadly. "My parents made me quit."

"What?" Lara shrieked. "You can't quit! You're my best friend in drama club! It won't be fun without you!"

Grace smiled. "You'll still have fun," she said.

"I guess that means that they found out, huh?"

"Yeah," Grace admitted. "I told them I was staying after school to study. They spoke to one of my teachers and he told them the truth." She looked closely at her friend. "The thing is . . ." she began, then paused.

"What is it, Grace?" Lara prompted. "You can tell me."

"I got some really bad grades in English last year,"

Grace said quietly. "My parents made me do all this reading over the summer, which I thought would make up for the bad grades. But they said I couldn't join drama because they didn't want me to fall behind in school again." She took a deep breath. It felt good to tell Lara the truth.

"Maybe I could help you," Lara suggested. "I'm not so good at math, but I'm good at English and history."

"You're not good at math?" Grace asked incredulously.

Lara laughed. "No way, Grace," she said. "I'm terrible, in fact."

"Wow," Grace said. "I sort of thought you were good at everything."

"So you have to quit the club right away?" Lara asked.

"Yeah. I have to go straight home." Grace checked her watch. "In fact, I have to leave now. My mom is coming home early to make sure I'm sticking to my punishment."

Lara sighed. "Okay, Grace. But I really do want to help you with English, if I can. If you'll let me, or if you want me to."

"I totally do," Grace replied honestly. "It would be fun!"

"It really would," Lara agreed. "Well, I'm really going to miss you today. Do you want to hang out over the weekend?"

"Grounded," Grace reminded her.

"Right. Well, I'll call you tomorrow anyway," Lara promised. "Just to say hi."

"Sounds good!"

"Talk to you then. Bye, Grace!"

"Bye, Lara. Have fun at drama club."

Despite not being allowed to participate in drama club, Grace was feeling cheerier. Lara knew her secret— that she wasn't a great reader—and it didn't make any difference in their friendship at all. As much as she would miss drama, she knew that having a new friend was much, much more important in the end.

▲ ▲ ▲

At home, Grace's mom was in the kitchen cooking. As Grace slid into her chair at the kitchen table, her mom plopped a full plate of apple slices and peanut butter in front of her.

"Mom, did I ever tell you about Chelsea from camp?" Grace said, digging into her plate of food.

"If I'm remembering correctly, she's the one who wasn't that nice, right?" her mom asked. She pulled a juice glass down from the cupboard and filled it with milk, which she set in front of Grace before sitting down across from her.

"Yeah. I mean, sometimes she could be snobby, but she wasn't that bad. Anyway, Julie, our counselor, posted this thing on the blog yesterday about Chelsea, and Julie said that Chelsea's dad is really sick."

"Oh no!" Grace's mom said, looking at her.

"Yeah. So we—all of us bunkmates, I mean—want to do something nice for her. I don't really know what to do, though."

"Well, whatever you decide on, I'm sure she'll appreciate it. That's a really sweet idea, and I'm sure you'll come up with something great, Grace," her mom replied.

She watched Grace eat for a moment. "Honey, I thought a lot about what happened last night."

Grace took a sip of her milk. "Me too, Mom," she said. "I'm really sorry for lying to you and to Dad. I just thought I could do it all."

"That's you, Grace," her mom said. "You *can* do it all, when you put your mind to it."

Grace picked up a slice of apple and popped it into her mouth. "This is really good," she said, with her mouth full.

"Your dad and I talked about it, and we've decided that you can stay in drama club," Grace's mom said.

Grace was shocked—so shocked, in fact, that she coughed and then nearly choked on her apple. For once, though, she wasn't joking around or trying to be dramatic. She was really that surprised! She swallowed quickly. "What?" she asked. "Are you serious?"

"Yes. You'll have to keep your B average, like we talked about, and if at the end of the semester you don't have a B average, you'll have to quit the club. But we really are proud of you for the hard work you've been doing so far this year. I know you can keep it up."

Grace couldn't believe how happy she was. "Oh, Mom, you won't regret this!" she cried. "Thank you!"

"You're still grounded for the week, with the exception of school and drama club," her mom went on. "And I am going to ask you to do some extra chores this weekend, which I'm sure you won't mind since you'll be here anyway," she said, winking.

Grace laughed. "I'd do anything to stay in drama club, Mom," she replied happily. "What do I have to do?"

"Well, the attic needs some cleaning out," her mom said, holding up one finger. She raised another finger. "And you'll do the dishes, and I'd like you to help me with the laundry on Saturday," she finished, holding three fingers in the air. "Think you can handle that, practice your drama club stuff, and do your homework?"

"Definitely, Mom," Grace said. She smiled. "My friend Lara is in drama club, and she said she'd help me with English. We can even study during our breaks!"

"That sounds great, Grace," her mom said. She smiled. "I'm still upset with you for lying to us, Grace," she went on. "But I know how important drama club is to you, and I don't think it will help you to take it away. Especially considering how much it motivated you to work hard."

"I'll keep working hard," Grace promised. She swallowed the rest of her milk and finished her last bite of apple.

Posted by: Grace
Subject: Drama club!

Hey, guys!
Crazy news!
My parents found out that I was lying to them about drama club, and they got really mad, but then this morning Mom told me that she was going to let me stay in it! She said she thought a lot about it and she is still mad at me for lying, and I'm grounded and have to do a bunch of chores and stuff, but I can stay in it!

And Lara offered to help me with some of my English

homework. She's so smart, and she's so cool, I bet she won't mind. And now I won't feel like I'm lying to her anymore.

I read some more of *The Pinballs* today. It's so good!

Talk to you later!

Love, Grace

ELEVEN

Jenna> FRIDAY

Jenna pounded on Nicole's front door at exactly seven fifteen, according to the Swatch watch her dad had bought her at the mall the weekend before. She was sweaty from running all the way to Nicole's house, and also, she supposed, a little nervous. While she waited for Nicole to answer the door, she glanced behind her, almost expecting to see her mom's car pulling into Nicole's driveway. *This has to work*, she thought frantically. *Because it's my only chance.*

Nicole swung the door open and pulled Jenna inside. "Hey!" she said. "I am so glad you could come!"

"Thanks!" Jenna said. "I can only stay till about nine or so. My mom could get back from my dad's any time after that."

"No problem," Nicole said. "There's a pizza coming in ten minutes, and we've got chips and soda. Everyone's downstairs."

"Awesome!" Jenna replied.

The two girls headed for the basement, where a movie was playing on the TV and a dozen kids were sitting in front of it eating chips and drinking soda.

"Look who's here!" Nicole announced. Everyone swiveled around to see Jenna and say hello.

"Hey, guys," Jenna said.

She and Nicole sat down to watch the movie. After a few minutes, Nicole's mom called down the stairs that the pizza was there, and Nicole went upstairs to get it. She brought back three pizza boxes, and everyone dug in, then went back to watching the movie.

After about half an hour of movie-watching, Jenna was starting to get pretty bored. She didn't know what the big deal was about Nicole's parties. So what if there were boys there? No one was even talking. *What this party needs is a fun party prank,* she thought. Even though she had promised not to pull them anymore, of course. Something needed to happen in order to liven things up. She didn't say anything, though, just kept watching the movie and chewing absent-mindedly on slice after slice of pizza. She wouldn't have had time to pull anything really great, anyway, so she let herself get swept up in the action on screen.

When the movie ended, Jenna realized that she must have been at Nicole's for two hours, and checked her watch. It was nine thirty. "Oh no!" she exclaimed.

"What's wrong?" a boy named Bobby said.

"I have to go home! My mom might be back already. She's going to kill me if she finds out that I snuck out!"

"You'd better hurry," Nicole said. "Do you want my mom to drive you?"

"No, she might tell my mom. I'll just run," Jenna

said. She stood up. "Bye, everybody." She ran up the stairs and out the front door, jogging through the neighborhood toward her house.

She couldn't believe it. She had risked getting into serious trouble—and for what? A lame party that wasn't even worth the effort. She could sit and watch movies (and eat pizza, too, for that matter) at her father's any time she wanted! But there was no way to turn back time, and so Jenna just continued to run as fast as she could, heart pounding all the way. *Please don't let Mom be home*, she thought. She knew it was a long shot, but it was the only chance she had.

She crossed her fingers as she ran. Just for good measure. She hoped it would help.

Å Å Å

When she got to her house, her heart sank—her mom's SUV was in the driveway, and the lights were on downstairs. She walked slowly up the pathway to her front door, dreading opening it. She slowly pushed the door open.

"Jenna?" her mom called from the kitchen.

"Yeah?" Jenna replied tentatively.

"Oh, thank God," Jenna's mom said, rushing into the living room. "I was so worried about you! I was about to call 911!"

"I'm okay," Jenna said quietly. She looked down at the floor, and then up at her mom.

The look on her mother's face changed from worry to confusion. "In that case, Jen, where have you been?" she asked pointedly.

"Um . . ." Jenna said, stalling for time.

"I mean it, young lady," her mom said, crossing her arms. "Where have you been? I was worried sick."

Jenna looked at the floor again and pretended to be interested in her shoes. "I went to Nicole's," she said quickly. "She was having a party." She looked at her mom out of the corner of her eye, and watched her mom's face turn red with anger.

"So you were only pretending to be sick," her mom said quietly.

"Yes," Jenna admitted. She looked her mother in the eye. "I'm sorry, Mom."

"You pretended to be sick so that you wouldn't have to go to your dad's, and so that you could sneak out and go to the party," her mom repeated.

"Yes."

"You've never been so grounded in your life," her mom said.

Jenna sighed. "Mom, this isn't fair, having to go to Dad's every weekend. I never get to do anything I want to do!"

"So you're missing out on your social life?" Jenna's mother asked angrily. "Jenna, this divorce isn't easy for any of us. And I can appreciate that it's rough on you kids—probably in ways your dad and I don't realize. But you are lucky to have two parents who love you so much. You are lucky to have a dad who wants to see you, and who looks forward to seeing you so much that he puts away his entire weekend for you and your brothers and sister." She shook her head. "You're lucky to have a dad who loves you so much," she finished.

"I know," Jenna said meekly. She moved her foot back and forth. "I love you and Dad, too." She thought about Natalie, who never got to see her dad because he was a famous movie star who was always in California working on movies. And then she remembered Chelsea.

"I'm so sorry, Mom," she blubbered. "I just thought—"

"You just thought you'd get away with it," Jenna's mom said. "Well, you almost did, Jen. Are you glad you got to go to the party? Was it worth it? You had me scared to death."

"Are you going to tell Dad?" Jenna asked softly.

Jenna's mom sighed. "I don't know," she admitted. "You lied to me, so this is between the two of us. On the other hand, you're obviously feeling very frustrated. I know you wouldn't have deceived me otherwise. So I think I am going to have to talk to him."

"Okay," Jenna said meekly. "You can tell him. It's okay. You can punish me, too. You can ground me or give me extra chores or whatever. I deserve it."

Jenna's mother laughed softly. "You do deserve it, Jenna—but just because you lied to me and snuck out of the house, which made me incredibly worried. I guess I didn't realize how much this was taking you away from your friends, and trust me, I know how important your friends are." She shook her head. "Maybe I'll talk to your dad about letting you guys all stay home one weekend a month, or something. Maybe he'd like to have you for Christmas, instead, and that can be the trade-off."

"Really?" Jenna replied hopefully. "It isn't that I don't like going to Dad's. It's just . . . I want to see my friends. And eat something other than pizza," she added.

Her mom laughed. "Really? What did you eat at Nicole's?"

Jenna laughed too. "Pizza," she admitted. "A bunch of it. The party was boring, too. It wasn't at all what I thought. I thought it'd be worth it."

"Come here, honey," her mom said, holding out her arms. "This will all work out."

Jenna walked toward her mom and wrapped her arms around her. They hugged for a moment, and then Jenna pulled back. "Mom?" she asked tentatively. "Would you take me to Dad's tonight?"

"No," her mom replied. "But I'll take you tomorrow morning. Tonight, why don't you and I watch a movie and eat some ice cream?"

"That sounds good," Jenna said.

"I miss you guys when you're gone, you know, Jen. And so does your father."

"I know," Jenna said. She followed her mom into the kitchen. From the freezer, her mom took out a pint of mint fudge ripple and Jenna grabbed two clean spoons. As they walked to the TV room, Jenna said, "My friend Chelsea's dad is really sick."

Jenna's mom looked sad. "Your friend from camp? How terrible."

"Yeah," Jenna replied. "I want to do something to help, but I don't know what."

"Did you e-mail her?"

Jenna settled into the couch and took the ice cream her mom handed her. "No," she said. "She wouldn't want that—she'd die if she thought anyone was feeling sorry for her." She was thoughtful for a second. "It's weird, that it didn't make me want to spend time with Dad when I first heard about it. I just felt bad for Chelsea, I didn't think about my own dad, who I'm lucky to have."

Jenna's mom smiled. "You're really growing up, Jen," she said. "I'm proud of you. I'm still mad at you for lying to me, skipping school, and sneaking out of the house, but you really are starting to grow up." She picked up the remote. "Want to watch something R-rated?" she asked.

"Seriously?" Jenna replied, surprised.

"No, not seriously," Jenna's mom said, laughing. "How about *Mean Girls*, though? I think you can handle that."

"Okay," Jenna said. She snuggled up to her mom as she turned on the TV and pressed Play on the DVD player.

"I was going to watch it myself," her mom confided. "But I'd much rather watch it with you."

SATURDAY

Posted by: Natalie
Subject: two weeks down . . .

hey, everybody. two weeks of school down, thirty-four to go! i'm having a pretty good time, but i do miss you guys. boys are confusing, friendships are hard work . . . and don't even get me started on how much more homework there is now that we are big old sixth-graders! i have been talking to simon on the phone, which is so cool. it's nice that just because we're not at camp doesn't mean we can't still get along just like we did then. minus the whole actually getting to see each other in person thing.

pluses about being back in nyc: cabs, air conditioning, hannah, clothes shopping, frappuccinos, central park. minuses: i miss you guys!

anyway, i wanted to update everyone, and to ask if you guys want to work on a project i came up with for a certain friend of ours. i want to keep it a secret, though, so e-mail me for details.

love, nat

Posted by: Grace
Subject: Grace's update

Hi! I think updates are a great idea. I've been cleaning the attic all morning (don't ask) and will start helping my mom with laundry after that. Plus I'm still grounded, plus I have tons of homework. But I get to stay in drama club, so that's good!

Nat, I'm in . . . I have some great ideas too!

Love, Grace

Posted by: Alex
Subject: Updates, updates, updates!

So . . . I went to the middle school football game last night with my friend Bridgette. And . . . drum roll please . . . there's this boy I think might like me! His name is Peter, and he held the door for me the other day (having crutches makes it hard to walk!).

He was at the game, and we sat together, and it got kind of cold so he gave me his sweater! It was so sweet. I don't know how I feel about boyfriends, but having a boy friend is great!

Speaking of friends, I definitely want to help, Natalie.
Love,
Al

Posted by: Jenna
Subject: Jenna's update

Hey, everybody. I'm at my dad's right now, and he's taking us to a movie in a bit so I don't have long. I'm really gr8ful 4 my dad right now. He talked to my mom and they agreed that 1 weekend a month, I'll stay at home 2 hang out with my friends. It'll be gr8. (I'm also gr8ful 4 my dad because he's just a gr8 dad in general!)

Let's all talk about the idea for u-know-who later today. I'll be on IM at about 6-ish. My IM screenname is Aries8 . . . talk to you then!
Love,
Jenna

Posted by: Julie
Subject: Great friends . . .

You guys are amazing.

Here's something else amazing: Camp Lakeview reunion, New York City, February!

More details coming soon . . . . . . get psyched!
Love, Julie

<Grrrrrace>: Hey, guys!

<Aries8>: Hey, Grace

<NatalieNYC>: it was cool to read everybody's updates today!

<SoccerLover>: Totally

<NatalieNYC>: sorry about yr leg alex :(

<SoccerLover>: Thanks! It's OK tho

<Aries8>: Does it hurt?

<SoccerLover: Not really

<NatalieNYC>: hey, grace, if you're grounded, how come u r online?

<Grrrrrace>: They would never ground me from the computer!

<Aries8>: LOL

<NatalieNYC>: so, did you guys hear about the reunion?!?!?!?!?!?!

<Aries8>: SO EXCITING!

<NatalieNYC>: i know, can't wait to show u new york city

<Grrrrrace>: i can't wait to see it!

<SoccerLover>: Me too. You'll have to give us the grand tour

<Aries8>: We can give Chelsea the present then, too

<Grrrrace>: What's your idea?

<NatalieNYC>: i luv presents . . .

<SoccerLover>: of course you do ;)

<Aries8>: Here's what I'm thinking . . . it'll be perfect!